# Teurith of Loring

by
## Koren Cowgill

## Artwork by
## Matt Jaffe

*Teurith of Loring*
© 2022 by Koren Cowgill
ISBN: 978-0-578-39867-9
Library of Congress Control Number: 2022905505

Printed in the United States of America

*Illustrations* © 2022 Matt Jaffe

*Book designed by SeaGrove Press*
*Ronald Thomas Rollet*

## Dedication

*For Mom and Dad*

## Acknowledgments

I thank those who took the time and energy to read drafts of Teurith of Loring including Richard, Sharon, Darlene, Mom and Dad, and Matt Jaffe. I thank Matt Jaffe for his stunning cover art and interior illustrations – bravo! I also thank Author Ron Rollet for making this book look beautiful and elegant. To my fellow writers: Ron, Steve, Jane, and Scott – I thank you for your ongoing support, suggestions, and compassion, and the writing and stories you share that inspire me so much.

# I

## *Dreams*
### *The Year 548*

Teurith scrambles up the hill, determined to finish mapping the north end of the Deafwood before Father misses her. The wood droops with hemlock trees; tall walnut, pine and oak trees stretch towards the sky. The forest floor, coated with pine needles, muffles the sound of Teurith's footsteps.

She glances behind her as Argo scratches the ground near a rabbit den in the brush along the path. "Hey, you," she calls, and throws her hair over her shoulder. He lifts his mammoth, black and brown head and sniffs the air, then looks back at the hole once before he catches up with her.

The sun sets, and in the dark of the forest, Teurith has trouble seeing the parchment. She sits on the root of an old, hoary oak tree, spreads the parchment on the uneven ground in front of her and takes the piece of coal out of her pocket. First, she draws a crude line representing the stream to where it meets the tree, and then a line north towards the field. She can make the map pretty later; for now, she focuses on major landmarks.

Her foot aches.

While Teurith swept the smithy floors a few weeks back, she stepped on a shard of metal, a scrap from a weapon her father forged. It went through her soft leather boot and into her foot. The boots are good for moving quietly through the forest, but the leather is thin. She can still feel the searing shock of hot iron on the bottom of her foot from when her father cauterized the wound. He knew what to do, and she endured it. She didn't scream, or even whimper. Father was the one who cried.

Father is the finest blacksmith in the Realm, specializing in the art of weapon making. The most ornate and finely crafted weapons come from his smithy in the village of Loring, from swords and battle axes, to knives, spears and flails. He also has the gift for magic like his father before him, and forges weapons with powerful crystal stones set into them. Men come from far away to request weapons made to order, and pay him well. Teurith is proud of him and although she does not want to follow his path, she helps him in the smithy when he allows it.

Teurith rolls the parchment and tucks it and the coal into her satchel. Argo trots after her as she limps down the hill away from the tree toward the stream. It'll be dark by the time they get home.

The Deafwood, named for the silence of the forest, is nestled in the foothills of the North Mountains and surrounds the village of Loring. Teurith and Argo stay on deer trails she knows well. In spite of the dark and quiet she isn't afraid. Argo leads the way, pausing every now and then to wait for Teurith, until she smells smoke from their chimney.

Light from the lantern outside the barn seeps through the trees. They find Father sitting on the bench in the yard, tamping tobacco in his pipe. He rises and Argo runs ahead to greet him, licking his hand with soft whines.

"Teury. I worried," Father says, voice low and stern. He scratches the dog behind his ears.

"I know the way. And Argo never leaves my side," she says, tosses her satchel on the bench and hugs her father.

"You mustn't linger in the forest beyond sunset. Old Coater's second-born grandson went out after dark to hunt rabbit and never came home."

"He probably ran away."

"Don't fool yourself, Child. The Tinker-folk pass through here when the rains come. They'll be here again before it turns cold and snows."

"I know that forest better than they do," Teurith says.

Her father blows rings of smoke into the air with a ghost of a smile. "It is said they sell children to the city dwellers."

"I know the stories. Tinker-folk don't scare me," she says.

He faces her, and rests his hands on her shoulders. "I must go to Riverton again."

Not much frightens Teurith—not the dark of the forest, not when Father burned her wound, and not being alone. Because she's only fourteen years old, father won't let her stay home on her own while he's away. Teurith frowns.

"What disturbs you?" Father says.

"Nothing."

"I won't be long. A fortnight, perhaps."

"That's an impossibly long time," she says.

"Come. It's late," he says. "We will speak more tomorrow."

She follows him inside.

Father is a burly man, tall and broad-shouldered. Unlike Teurith, he doesn't have a thick, black mane of hair. His hair is thinning, and he keeps his blond, bearded face trimmed.

Built of stone and wood of oak, their home is larger than the usual village dwelling, with two rooms for sleeping, each with its own fireplace, and a common area with a metal stove, the only one of its kind north of Riverton.

Teurith's father built their home not long after her birthing. In return for her father's services, King Egad of Riverton gave him land in Loring and compensated him with blocks of stone and other building materials for their dwelling and the smithy. The King had them delivered to Loring, twenty leagues northwest of the city. When her father finished building, he brought Teurith home. That was ten years ago.

Teurith often wonders where she was born. "I'll tell you when you're old enough," Father always said. By the light of the lantern, she takes the scroll of parchment from her satchel and stacks it with the others. Too tired to unroll and fit them together to see how her map looks, she dresses for nighttime. She extinguishes the light, climbs in bed, and stares at the thick, wooden beams above. Argo jumps up with her, yawns and stretches out by her feet.

Teurith has fragmented memories from when she lived in the other place with walls of stone and windows too high for her to see out. She remembers a woman with merry eyes and a belly laugh who cared for her before she came to live with Father. She still hears the woman's laugh, and that makes Teurith smile. She recalls the chamber with the fireplace. Although she was too tiny to see anything out the windows but the sky, Teurith had the feeling the ground was far below.

She drifts off to sleep, and dreams.

*Teurith runs, following the narrow deer path through the dim wood. She's been here before, running, running, running, her tattered clothes blowing about her. They're chasing her and although they're way behind, Teurith continues, darting glances over her shoulder. Her pants stick to her skin, soaked with blood, and keep her from running faster. She doesn't know why she bleeds. She feels dirty—not just her clothing. Her mind closes to shut out the hateful things they did to her. Exhausted, she finally slows and stops, staring into the darkness in front of her.*

"No, no, please." Teurith tries to scream, and wakes with her heart thumping too fast. She squeezes her eyes shut.

"Teury. It's just a dream." Father leans over her, and places his hand on her forehead. "You are not well. You must have a fever." He leaves the room, soon returns with a damp cloth and places it on her forehead.

"Thank you, Father." After he leaves, Teurith turns on her side, and holds the cool cloth to her face. Sleep won't come again and she stares at the window until the dawn emerges through the dark night.

In the light of day while sitting at table with Father, Teurith relaxes.

"How do you feel this morning? And how are your maps?" Father asks, reaching over to place his palm on her forehead.

"I'm well."

He furrows his brow. "You were full of heat and your face was clammy. I am still concerned."

"Don't fret, Father. And the map will be huge when I fit it all together. Someday, when I am grown, I'll make maps for the King. For now, I'll map the Deafwood. I have one more to make before I finish the north end of it."

"Will you fashion a map of the village?"

"There's no need. It's small and everyone knows where they're going."

"It would be useful for strangers passing through," Father says.

"I suppose so." A twinge of fear nags at her. "Must I stay at the Inn? Can I go with you to Riverton this time?"

"You always enjoy staying at the Inn with Lord Magus. He's our good friend. And I must deliver flails to Riverton. I will leave in two days and do my best to return quickly."

"I'm sorry, Father. It's just—lately I have been having dreams…"

He raises his eyebrows. "Like the one last night? What are they about?"

"Yes. I dream that I'm running, and someone's chasing me, but I don't know who."

"Teury. They're only dreams."

"Can I please go with you to Riverton this time?" she says.

"No. When you're older, perhaps."

"You say that about everything. Like when you wouldn't let me call Argo Grunkus and never told me why you call him Argo." She laughs.

Father smiles. "Such a dog needed a hero's name. Remember when I brought him home to you five years ago?"

She nods. "He was just a puppy—from King Gareth's kennels in Riverton. But who's Argo?"

"Well," he says and pauses. "He was a lord in King Gareth's father Egad's court, and also a knight of high stature in the King's army—a great warrior."

"A warrior?" she asks.

"His name was Argo." He hesitates. "I knew him."

Teurith's eyes widen. "Great stags! How did you know him?" She leans forward in her seat.

"I grew up in Riverton."

"You never told me," Teurith says. She frowns and looks away.

"I am sorry. I knew you would have questions, and wanted to delay answering."

"Why?"

"Because that's where you lived for a time as well, after your birthing," he says, quiet and cautious.

Teurith remains silent. She doesn't want to know any more. Father must leave soon and she'll stay at the inn. The owner of the Village Boar Inn is Father's friend, a minor lord called Magus Longwell. He's a kind, prosperous man who gives Teurith chores to complete during her stay and rewards her for her efforts.

But now, she doesn't want to go there. Argo can't even go with her. Father takes him on the journey to Riverton and he runs with Father's horse Kaspar beside the wagon and the six carthorses. And that's only—

"Teurith?" Father says.

"I was thinking." She smooths her shirt and tucks it into her trousers. "I need to finish my chores so I can get to the Deafwood."

"Would you like me to go with you today?"

"No, thank you. I'll be home by mid-afternoon."

"Don't be late. Chores before you go, and give Kaspar a bit of a run."

"Yes, Father."

Teurith gives the horses their grain and mucks the stalls. Kaspar nuzzles the small of her back as she spreads fresh hay on the floor. "Oh, you—giant lug of a horse." She laughs quietly, grateful for animals, and finishes her task. "C'mon, Kaspar; let's ride."

Kaspar whinnies and clomps to the gate. Teurith steps up the rungs of it so she's high enough to climb on Kaspar's back. He noses the gate open; she grasps his mane, gives him a squeeze with her legs and they take off.

Her father's land, just northeast of Loring, stretches over rolling, meadowed hills near the Deafwood. Teurith and Kaspar gallop along the edge of the wood until they come to the North Road, then turn around and head for home. She laughs into the breeze, her hair flying behind her. They arrive and Kaspar trots into the enclosure. He neighs and the carthorses run to his call.

"Good horse, Kaspar," Teurith says. She swings her leg over him and allows herself to slip to the ground, surrounded by Kaspar and the other horses. "Take care of Father on the way to Riverton." She pulls an acorn cap from her pocket, fits her thumbs on either side of it and blows hard, a shrill whistling sound echoing through the morning mist.

The horses disperse and move towards the stable. Argo appears by the barn, wagging his tail with his tongue hanging out the side of his mouth. "Let's go, my friend," she says, and they trot up the path, leaving home behind them.

Today they follow the stream to the meadow. A few yards beyond the large oak tree where they've rested before, the ground levels out for a few paces, then drops off. Teurith is careful not to fall as she negotiates a series of ravines. She's avoided this part of the Deafwood until now because of its steepness. She counts her paces from the oak tree to the first ravine and eases herself along, continuing to count. They reach the bottom. She pauses, gazing up at the tops of trees as flecks of late morning light filter through them.

Towering trees give way to thick brush and even hillier terrain as they approach the northern edge of the Deafwood, the North Mountains looming above. Teurith expects to hear sounds from the North Road that winds between forest and mountains. There is only quiet, and when she looks for Argo, she sees him standing still with his tail at attention, sniffing the air. Then she smells it, too, smoke from a recently abandoned campfire.

She thinks of the Tinker-folk; they come with the rain from the north in late autumn and it's only high summer. Something tells her to turn and head home. She ignores it and continues moving forward, counting her paces. Argo walks by her side.

The smell grows stronger and they come to a small clearing where curls of smoke still rise from a makeshift fire pit. Argo stands rigid and tense, a low growl in his throat. He stays at the edge of the clearing and doesn't move as Teurith studies the ground around the fire. He whines. Teurith steps back from the fire and sees jagged markings on the ground. She doesn't know what they mean, but the symbols are misshapen letters rather than the text she learned to read from Father's scrolling crystals. She places her hand on her forehead, and dizziness overwhelms her.

*Darkness floods the clearing, and lightening flares around Teurith. As she stands shaking, a woman appears, throws her head back and laughs, her wispy gown and golden curls fluttering around her. The markings on the ground glow, etched deep into the earth with blood and brimstone. Teurith's heart pounds, her feet rooted where she stands. Then sunlight brightens the clearing and the ground swallows the symbols; the earth shudders as they disappear. The woman is gone.*

Teurith recovers and runs with Argo at her side. She uses roots of trees and bushes to pull herself out of the final ravine and onto the level ground above, until they're well into the Deafwood. Somehow, they stray from the path. She needs to get home. Father expects her by mid-afternoon. But she doesn't know the way.

Light fades and branches lash her face as she struggles to find a trail. Argo whimpers and stops. Teurith plops on the ground beside her dog. It's dark and an eerie fog develops. Argo leans against her as the mist swallows them. She forces her mind to focus. Even the trees appear frightening, twisted and gnarled. She closes her eyes and imagines light, a bright light. With her eyes still shut, she concentrates. The thick, damp air surrounding Teurith and Argo chills them. The dog shakes and Teurith pulls her cloak around them as she shivers.

She squints into the woods and sees a distant glow. It approaches them, and Teurith stands. Hundreds of fireflies form a halo around her. They brighten so Teurith and Argo can find their footing.

"Great stags," Teurith whispers, peering into the light in front of her. She continues to trudge forward, careful to push back branches so they won't hit her face or Argo's, all the while trying to keep her balance. "But can we move faster?" she says to the glowworms.

Teurith hears a cacophony of hooting. Three owls fly out of the brush in front of them, hover for a moment, and turn and fly in the direction of the glow, slow enough to allow Teurith and Argo to keep up.

"Hello?" Teurith says, and quickens her pace. She smiles at the white fluff beneath the owls' ruffled tailfeathers. The fog starts to clear and eventually she sees the lights of her home flickering in the distance. She runs faster, stumbles into the clearing and sees her father holding a lantern up into the night.

Father approaches. "Teurith," he says, his face darkening and he takes her in his arms.

Teurith glances behind her, fireflies and owls nowhere to be seen.

"It is dark again and you're only now home. Why this behavior?" He releases her and touches her forehead. "You're feverish again. Have some broth and go to bed."

"Father."

"Yes, Child."

"I got us lost. But the fireflies and owls came, and led us here, and—"

"Now, Teury. This is serious. Once more, you are late. I have had enough. You must sleep. Your dreams must come from these wild imaginings."

"But they were real. Please let me come with you, please Father."

He takes her hand in both of his. "I can take you with me soon. But not until your sixteenth name day."

"Why? That's over a year away," she cries, and yanks her hand out of his.

"Hush, Teury. Please. Understand."

"But I don't understand and want to know now."

His face reddens and he raises his voice. "You cannot know now. You mustn't."

She lowers her head.

He sighs. "I am sorry, Teury. There are reasons. Try to understand."

Teurith nods and sulks her way to her room, Argo trailing behind her. She spreads her map of the Deafwood out on the table, and traces the lines she's drawn. "Now to make it look better. But how?" She moves to the wardrobe and pulls a bundle of cloth from under her clothes. She unwraps the cloth and takes one of the three crystals.

The blue crystal is for reading the histories of The Realm since the time of

Queen Benadras, the gold one, a collection of stories with illuminated drawings. The green crystal is her favorite, the one with the maps. As she holds the green crystal into the moonlight, it expands into a tablet in her hands. She scrolls through until she finds the map of The Realm. The landmarks are small but it gives her an idea of how to enhance her own maps.

She smiles and thinks of her father, who taught her to read the scrolling crystals.

"This is a gift, Teury. Most never learn to read," he always said.

"Thank the gods for Father. And you, too, Argo," Teurith says as she scratches the dog's head. He wags his tail then settles down in a corner. She yawns and returns the crystals to the wardrobe, then curls herself on the bed, the sound of Argo's steady snoring easing her fears. She sleeps and dreams of glowworms and owls leading her to safe havens.

# II

## *Racing to the Wall*
### *The Year 532*

PRINCESS Egrith peers in the window, watching Dirk sweep the floor. She's careful not to let him see her, but hears everything going on inside because the smithy door is open. Dirk works to the clanking of metal on metal while his father Derrek, Royal Blacksmith of Riverton, forges another broadsword. Egrith admires Dirk's muscled arms, imagining how it would feel if they held her close.

Derrek pounds the sword on the anvil with a hammer, then turns to his son. "Now, hold the hammer and strike the bottom of the sword near the hilt."

Dirk lets the hammer hover above the sword for a moment, hits it once, then again.

"That's good. Slow and steady." Derrek stands back from Dirk and smiles. "Now cool the blade."

Egrith hears the hot metal hiss on the water.

Dirk stretches, removes his leather apron, and hangs it on a hook, then returns to the broadsword and runs his fingers over the flat of the blade. "Father, who will wield such a weapon? The enormous hilt is made for two hands."

"I hear the King's new commander of the guard, Lord Krimpt, is of a height and breadth to handle this blade." Derrek wipes his hands on his apron. "That is all for now. I will finish the jewel work on the hilt myself later."

Dirk glances toward the door. "I can go now?"

"Yes. Be back for supper," Derrek says.

Egrith stays quiet as Dirk stands still for a moment before he reaches the doorway. She smiles at his new beard. His blue eyes are large and striking on his tanned face. Dirk walks to his father for a moment and Egrith retreats farther out of sight, then feels a tug on her sleeve.

"Hello, dear Sister."

"Oh, Gareth. Shhh. Let's surprise him."

Dirk returns, moves through the doorway and Gareth tackles him. The two young men wrestle and Gareth pins Dirk to the ground on his stomach.

Egrith places her hands over Dirk's eyes just as Argo arrives, and he says, "Guess who?"

"Well I know it's you, Argo. I may be stuck under Gareth but I'm not deaf," Dirk says, laughing.

"It's me," Egrith says.

Dirk struggles out of Gareth's stronghold and reddens.

Princess Egrith dances around him, giggling. A green tunic with a fitted bodice tucked into brown riding leggings flatters her figure, already blossomed into maturity at her almost sixteen years of age. Dirk is also about to turn sixteen, their friend Argo and her brother Prince Gareth, already seventeen.

"Princess," Dirk says, and bows.

"Oh, please don't do that," she says, and stops laughing. "Egrith."

"I'll never get used to it," Dirk says.

"We're friends and that's that. I only have you three."

"You'd have Margrin and the ladies of the court if you didn't follow us around all day," Gareth says. "We thought we'd come and find you this morning, Dirk."

Prince Gareth is the tallest, lean with light brown hair. Dirk is almost as tall but burlier. Argo has black hair, blue eyes and a thin frame like Egrith, only he is taller than she.

Dirk pretends to look around the corner, then bolts down the lane. "Race you to the stables!"

"Not fair." Egrith runs after him.

"He'll never make it there before my sister," Gareth says. "She knows every shortcut, every alleyway—and she's fast."

Argo laughs. "C'mon," he says, and they follow.

Egrith sees Dirk ahead of her. While he continues down Smithy Lane, she takes a right through a narrow passageway, a shortcut leading to High Road. That will bring her to the river bridge at the main gate of the castle before he reaches it.

The stables are at the southeast corner of the wall surrounding the castle, beyond the kennels. Egrith slows and passes through the stable entrance. Stalls line either side of the large stone barn. One of the stable boys holds a horse's leg steady as the court farrier shoes it. Egrith waves at him and he smiles. She continues until she reaches the last stall, where the King's warhorse Kraken lives. Kraken scuffs his feet and snorts as Egrith approaches him. She opens the gate of his stall, pats the horse's neck and moves behind a stack of haybales.

"Egrith?" Dirk says.

She stifles a giggle, and hears Dirk's footfalls coming closer until he stands in front of the stall where Egrith hides.

Kraken clomps to the gate, shakes his head and whinnies.

"You are a huge, strapper of a horse, aren't you?" Dirk says, stroking Kraken's mane.

"Thank you, Dirk," Egrith says in her best horse voice. She neighs and giggles again, then appears from behind the stack of hay bales.

"I knew you had to be here," Dirk says.

"Couldn't resist." Egrith smiles and tosses her black ponytail over her shoulder where it hangs to her waist.

Egrith's eyes pierce Dirk's.

He looks down and scratches at the stubble on his chin. "I'm easy game; you get me every time. Will you ride Kraken today?"

"Father doesn't want me to. But you won't tell, will you."

"He's a big horse, even for me," Dirk says. "I stand two hands taller than you and I couldn't handle him."

"Don't fret. The Kraken adores me, don't you my Dearie," she says and kisses the horse's nose.

Gareth and Argo approach. "Saddle up," Gareth says, and strides down the length of the last few stalls.

The four friends mount their horses, ride to the east gate and beyond castle and city walls. They turn south, and after riding a few minutes past Riverton, they head west. Gareth and Argo travel ahead and Dirk keeps apace with Egrith. They gallop over rolling fields to the northern edge of Lightbane Forest.

"When Cook wasn't looking I managed to convince Emmet to make us a basket for lunch," Egrith says.

"Those kitchen boys would do anything for you," Dirk says.

"That's not so. He only made the basket because I promised him I'd look for whitetail root as we explore today. Cook likes to season Father's beef dishes with it. It's a rare root."

"It is true. We'd all take an arrow for you."

"Well, I'd do the same for you," she says.

They continue along the forest until they see the stream sparkling through the trees in the sunlight. Argo and Gareth have already tied their horses to trees by the time Egrith and Dirk arrive.

"Great Gods, Egrith. What did you bring?" Gareth says, pulling Egrith's bundle off the back of her horse.

"Oh, lunch. And a few crystals."

"Why?" Gareth says.

Dirk groans.

Egrith nods and says, "We have to keep up with your reading, Dirk. Don't you like it?"

"I like it well enough. It's tiring," he says.

"You'll be grateful for it later."

"Uh-huh." Dirk moves towards Egrith as she swings one leg over Kraken and slides off before he can help her dismount.

Argo slings a quiver over his shoulder. "Gareth and I will hunt and you two can guard the horses."

"Behave yourselves," Gareth says.

Argo blushes and glances at Egrith and Dirk, who already sit between the roots of a lofty walnut tree with a scrolling crystal in front of them. He joins Gareth and they head toward the forest.

"Fah-fah-vor-ed," Dirk says.

"Favored. The king's features favored."

"Oh. Favored. The king's features—favored—his mother, Queen Ben-Ben-a-dras."

"Good," she says and squeezes his arm. "You're getting quicker." Egrith sees redness on Dirk's neck and smiles.

"His mane of cuh-uh-rrrls han-guh—hangs below his neck."

"Yes. Mane of curls hangs below his neck. Dirk?"

"Yes?"

"Do you—never mind."

"What?" he says.

Egrith hesitates. "This is silly. But—do you think—do you think I'll ever be as pretty as Margrin?"

Dirk laughs before he can help himself.

"I'm happy you find me so amusing," she says.

"Sorry. Uh, well. Margrin? She's not fit to please anyone with her nose high in the air and her sour face. And she—"

"What?"

"She wears a scent that turns my stomach, or maybe it's just her smell."

"Her smell." Egrith wrinkles her nose.

"I haven't gotten close enough to tell for sure. Except that one time, when I delivered a jeweled ax to the captain of the guard for father. She was walking down the lane and wouldn't smile at me as we passed; that smell trailed behind her."

"You're lucky. I'm stuck with her. The older boys like her. But apart from the smell and the sour puss, is she pretty?"

Dirk stands, looking north so she won't see his face. "None of them could ever hold a flame to you."

Egrith's heart leaps, and she opens another scrolling crystal. Dirk sits again and they continue reading.

"You are right to pronounce each syllable slowly until you finish such a big word."

"In-ex-tric-a-bleh-bleh-ble. What does that mean?"

"It means—this is hard—it means, impossible to separate. Like, the four of us are inextricably connected to one another."

"I still don't understand," Dirk says, shaking his head.

"We're friends. We met and became fast friends, like we'd already known each other."

"And it's like we'll be friends forever?" he says.

"Yes. Grena says we live again and again, and have the same friends from one lifetime to the next."

Dirk stays quiet and runs his fingers over the smooth crystal tablet. Then they read his favorite gold crystal, stories of knights who slay frightening creatures and of great foreign warriors. Illuminated pictures of brilliant colors accompany the stories. The sun sets lower in the sky, and shines through the trees as Gareth and Argo arrive, a felled rabbit slung over Gareth's shoulder.

"Have you been doing that all of this time?" Argo asks.

"We're just finishing. It's too late for a fire. My brother, we have to arrive in time for dinner with father. You can give the rabbit to Cook," Egrith says.

"Just as well. But dinner will be much later and we're hungry now," Gareth says.

Egrith spreads a throw on the ground and takes fruit, bread and cheese from the basket. Everyone gorges on the food except for Dirk, who remains still, looking out over the meadow.

"Let's have a game," Gareth says.

Dirk groans again. "Not Say or Act."

"That's a good idea, Dirk," Argo says, and laughs. "We have four hours of daylight. No sense getting back before dusk."

Gareth stands. "Okay. We'll draw sticks to see who asks the first question, or commands an act." He finds four sticks and breaks them to different lengths, then holds them in his hand. "Whoever draws the longest gets to go first."

Egrith draws first, and huffs because the stick is short. Dirk draws second, a stick that is longer than Egrith's. Gareth's stick looks much like Dirk's and Argo draws the longest one.

"Ha. I go first," Argo says. "Dirk. Say or Act."

Dirk hesitates. "I choose to Say."

Argo smirks and says, "Who is the prettiest lady of the castle?"

Dirk's forehead beads with sweat, and he smooths hair out of his eyes. "Um," he begins, and keeps himself from glancing at Egrith, "Queen Benadras. We just saw and read about her in the crystal."

"What a lame answer. She's been dead almost five-hundred years," Gareth says.

"Oh, leave him be," Egrith says, and moves closer to Dirk.

"I'll go again; that wasn't fair," Argo says. "Gareth. Will you say or Act."

Gareth squints into the distance and says, "Act."

"I command you to—ride fast to the Barkus Wall, and jump it."

"Neither king nor knight crosses the Barkus Wall," Gareth quotes.

"It's said there are magic barriers built into the wall," Egrith says. "And it's too high in most places for a horse to jump. You have to climb it."

"And father says to stay away from it. Strange things happen to those who do cross," Gareth says. "But let's ride out and see it before we return to the castle."

"Best we head for home. My father will worry, and you three have to be at court," Dirk says.

"Let's just see," Egrith says, a gleam in her eye.

The four friends ride along the edge of the forest until they see the wall standing on the horizon. They run the horses hard, then the wall stands taller, in full view.

Gareth pulls on his horse's reins. "The Barkus Wall spans from Lightbane Forest to the Sounding Sea, only twenty leagues. Its construction began upon Queen Benadras' orders five-hundred years ago."

"Why?" Dirk says.

Egrith moves Kraken alongside Dirk's horse. "The wall is meant to warn people who don't mean well. At the time of Queen Benadras, those who practiced the darker aspects of the Barkus Arts were banished to the desert lands south of the wall. They say sorcerers with ill intent will die if they touch it."

Egrith, swift and sudden, pulls on Kraken's reins, then digs her heels into his side. The horse takes off. She pounds Kraken harder and harder as he races towards Barkus Wall.

"Egrith," Dirk shouts, slaps his mount with a switch and charges after Egrith.

"Dirk, no," Gareth says, and raises his voice. "Your horse will never make it." He runs his horse after Dirk.

Argo follows and watches as Egrith and Kraken disappear over the wall in a shimmer of haze.

Dirk gallops faster. His horse reaches the wall and stops just short of it, throwing Dirk to the ground.

Argo dismounts and runs to Dirk, then kneels on the ground beside him.

"Dirk!" Gareth says. He bends over Dirk and feels his forehead. "He's not moving, and he's clammy."

"He had quite a fall," Argo says. "Stay with him. I worry for Egrith." He walks to the wall. "Eee-grith." When she doesn't answer, Argo turns back toward Dirk and Gareth. "Dirk?"

"Egrith," Dirk slurs.

"Can you stand?" Gareth says.

"Is she here? My head—woozy—and I feel numb."

Gareth and Argo stand over him.

"Can we help you get up?" Argo says.

"Egrith," Dirk says again.

"We'll find her. Give us your arms and we'll pull you up," Gareth says.

They help Dirk rise and once he's standing, they hear laughter echoing through the mist, a tinkling sort of laughter.

"Hello-oh," Egrith says, her voice faint.

Dirk exhales, slumps between Argo and Gareth, and they lay him on the ground again. Dirk closes his eyes.

Kraken leaps over the wall and Egrith dismounts, then runs to Dirk. "Oh!" she says, sits next to Dirk, and cradles his head in her lap.

He opens his eyes. "You're here," he says.

"I jumped the wall," Egrith says. "But, oh, I am sorry, my friend. You're hurt."

"You scared me—didn't know if you'd make it," Dirk says.

"I knew the Kraken wouldn't let me fall. We must get you home safely."

Gareth gazes at his sister. "You shouldn't have done that. And it was a treacherous dare," he says, turning to Argo.

"I didn't think anyone would actually do it," Argo says.

"My head hurts," Dirk says.

"It's getting dark. He can ride with me," Gareth says.

Egrith places her hand on Dirk's forehead. "He's hot, like he has a fever."

"We'd best get on, then," Argo says.

They ride until after dark. When they reach the east gate, a guardsman and Dirk's father, Derrek, greet them. "The King summons you, Lady Egrith, and you, Prince Gareth, to his quarters," the guard says.

Derrek moves to Gareth's horse, where Dirk sits behind the prince. He helps his son down and they enter the castle gate.

Gareth and Egrith follow the guardsman.

Argo stands alone, and watches them walk away.

# III
## *The Inn*
### *The Year 548*

TEURITH stands beside Lord Magus Longwell and watches her father's back as he rides Kaspar, posting in his saddle; the carthorses know to follow Kaspar's lead. Argo pauses to look back at Teurith once before he continues trotting alongside her father and the carthorses. They finally disappear around the bend.

The sound of their clip-clopping fades and Teurith glances up at Lord Magus. He takes her hand. Tall like her father, he's thinner with dark hair to his shoulders, brown eyes and a thin mustache.

"Let me take your rucksack to your room," Magus says, and smiles.

Teurith follows him into the inn and through the dining area to the stairway, where they climb to the third floor.

He opens a door at the end of the hall. "Please let me know if you need anything. I'm just down the hallway."

"Thank you, Magus. I will."

She takes her clothes, stows them in a dresser drawer and lays her favorite green scrolling crystal on the table. One window overlooks the gardens; the other, the stables. She opens a window and inhales. The combined scents of flowers and horses calm her.

Magus returns. "Oh, Teurith. Would you like to help me in the gardens today?"

"I would," she says.

"Will you break your fast with me first?"

"That will be nice." She follows him to the kitchens.

Two scullery maids busy themselves at the sink washing dishes.

"Sandrine, fetch eggs, enough for Teurith and me, and some for you and Callie," Magus says.

Sandrine jumps at the sound of his voice, then giggles as she and Callie curtsy and blush.

"And you remember Teurith. She'll be with us again for a couple of weeks."

"Hello, again," Teurith says. She smiles at the girls' blushes. Magus is handsome, and he's kind to everyone.

The girls curtsy and continue washing.

"Let's collect some spinach to have with the eggs," Magus says.

He leads her to the back exit of the inn and into the gardens beyond. Dragonflies flit among the bean poles, their transparent wings alight with rays of morning sun. Flowers, varied and colorful, blanket the yard in the midst of the different vegetables. Magus pulls a bunch of spinach from the ground and Teurith collects another.

"I have a task for you if you want to keep busy," he says.

She bends to inhale the scent of one of the flowers, and waits for him to speak.

"I would like you to be in charge of making the inn beautiful," he says.

"Good," she says.

"You are welcome to choose flowers you like to place around the inn. Sandrine will make vases ready, and will help you with garlands for stairway and windows."

"I would love to."

"The inn will be full in a few days. More servants will come tomorrow to help ready the rooms. For now, work on the flowers, and otherwise pass the time as you wish."

Teurith helps Callie set the table as Sandrine prepares a breakfast of omelets with spinach. Magus joins them and they sit at the table; the girls continue to giggle among themselves, stealing glances at Magus, and Teurith relaxes enough to eat her food.

Sandrine and Callie clear the table and Teurith and Magus rise from their chairs. "Thank you, girls," Magus says.

Days pass and Teurith enjoys making garlands, twisting stems of flowers together to form long strands accented by blooms of daisies and zinnias. When she isn't working she sits in a corner of the garden reading the Histories in the blue scrolling crystal. One afternoon, as Sandrine picks pods of peas, a smell tingles Teurith's nose—not a foul smell, but spicy and pungent. She ignores it and focuses on the story. Tales of war and magic fill her head.

"What are you doing, and what is that?" Sandrine says as she husks the peas.

"It's a crystal, see?" Teurith runs her hand over the tablet and it shrinks into a tablet that fits in one hand. Then, she moves her fingers over it again and it expands. She shows Sandrine how the words materialize as the story scrolls.

"Magic," Sandrine says, and backs away.

"Don't be afraid. It is magic, but not a bad sort of magic."

Sandrine leans over the tablet. "What are those symbols?"

"They're letters that form words you can read. This is a history of a time way before King Egad, when Queen Benadras ruled."

"A queen? I thought we only had kings."

"Well, we do have kings sometimes. Long ago, King Fernand died at the hand of the last, dark practitioner of the Barkus arts remaining in the northern lands. His queen, Benadras, banished the witch-man south to the Desert Lands. She had magical abilities herself, and built the Barkus wall of magic crystal and stone."

Sandrine shivers. "I heard tell all magic is evil."

Magus arrives and says, "Not true."

Sandrine gazes at Magus, blushes and continues her work.

Teurith follows Magus into the inn.

Light fades as dusk approaches. Teurith reads, sitting at one of the long tables in the dining room. Sandrine and Callie are in their room for the night, and Magus is nowhere to be seen.

Knock, knock.

Teurith jumps in her seat.

Knock, knock, knock.

She hears a scratching sound outside the main door of the inn, and looks towards the stairway. Magus doesn't appear and she hears voices.

She rises and approaches a window by the door, then peers into the dim lantern light. She sees three tall, slender figures in the misty rain. Before they knock again, Teurith opens the door.

"We seek Lord Magus Longwell," a woman says. She pulls her hood away, her clear, green eyes bright, and she smiles at Teurith.

"He's not here—might be in the stables." Teurith holds the door open, making room for them to enter.

The women walk past her.

Teurith closes the door and calls after them, "Would you like some tea or water?"

The green-eyed woman stops. "Yes, a hot tea would be lovely. The nights are getting colder."

Teurith stares at them as they remove their cloaks and sit at the table.

"What is it, dear?" the green-eyed woman says, and removes her hair from a clip, letting long auburn curls flow over her shoulders.

Teurith hesitates. "I—I've never seen anyone so beautiful. Your clothes—they give off their own light—and your hair…"

The woman laughs. "Thank you." She smooths her shimmery silver dress over her knees.

Teurith moves to the kitchen and puts the kettle on. When she brings the tea to the common area she finds Magus talking with the women. "…the pack horse to the stables and I'll return directly," he says.

"All in good time," the woman says, then addresses Teurith. "And what is your name?"

"Teurith," she says. "Did you travel far?"

"We are always moving, rarely stay in one place for long."

"Like the Tinker-folk?" Teurith says before she can stop herself.

The woman smiles. "The Tinkers are known to wander some. Most of the time they travel the same routes throughout the year."

"Oh."

The other women talk in hushed whispers, sipping their tea.

"Ma'am?"

"Yes?"

"What's your name?"

"Yana, and these are my companions, Morin and Tendris."

Teurith rises from the bench, pushing herself up with her palms on the table.

"May I?" Yana says and takes Teurith's hand. She turns it over so the palm is facing up.

Teurith tries to pull away.

"All is well."

Yana's voice soothes Teurith.

She traces the lines on Teurith's palm with her fingers. "The palm is square, and the fingers shorter than the length of the palm from wrist to fingers."

"What does that mean?" Teurith says.

"You have the hand of fire."

Teurith steps back.

"Stay."

Teurith doesn't move.

The other two women become quiet, listening, and then chat again as Yana traces the curved line from under Teurith's index finger to below her little finger. "The line of your heart is long, and already becoming crossed with care. Under it, the head line is straight, and formed between the thumb and index finger to the middle of your palm below the little finger."

"What does that tell you?"

"You are a creator with keen thirst for knowledge."

"What about the other hand?"

"The lines are deep, and etched with trial."

Magus returns from the stables, and gives Teurith the opportunity to stand.

Yana's eyes pierce Teurith's and then she says, "We must retire and sleep. I will finish the palm reading another time."

"Yana, may I show you the gardens after breakfast tomorrow?" Teurith says.

"Yes. Rest well."

"Good night, ladies," Magus says.

Once settled in her room Teurith lies still in her bed, but sleep won't come. Deep and etched with trial. That's what Yana said of the other hand, the one she doesn't write with. She thinks of her father, so far away. Finally, she sleeps until the morning sun wakes her.

Callie and Sandrine serve breakfast. Because there are guests at the inn, they'll break their morning fast in the kitchen after the company has eaten. Teurith and Magus eat with the women.

Teurith pokes at her food and glances around the room at the other guests, mostly weary looking men who travel the North Road through the mountains and stop in Loring on their way to Riverton. One man who sits in the far corner of the dining room catches her attention. Teurith eyes the longsword strapped to his back and shivers. Greasy hair hangs over his forehead as he slurps his porridge.

Yana follows Teurith's gaze. "There is no reason for alarm. That is Knut. He travels with us at times, but prefers to keep his own company."

"I didn't see him last night."

"He does not sleep indoors," Yana says, and pats Teurith's hand. "We are ready to see the garden."

Teurith leads Yana and the other two women to the garden, and she points to the flowers she chose to fashion the garlands.

"Beautiful. Now, show me the herbs."

In a corner of the yard where she usually reads her scrolling crystals, different greens straggle out of the ground. Yana stoops to one of the herbs. "This is Bellam's Root, a remedy that soothes the unquiet soul."

"That's the one that smells," Teurith says and leans closer to the plant.

"Herbs that carry strong remedies often have a unique odor."

"Oh."

"Come to my room after dinner. I have a mixture that will help you rest."

"Thank you."

After the evening meal Teurith helps Sandrine and Callie clear the tables and wash the dishes. It's dusk when the girls retire. Teurith follows them up the stairs and then continues to her room.

In the quiet of the inn, Teurith wonders whether she should go to Yana's room after all. She blows the candle out and sits on the edge of her bed. A sweet fragrance drifts through her window and as she inhales, it begins to slow her breathing, helping her grow calm.

She leaves her room, then moves into the hallway and down the stairs. On the first floor where the women have their rooms, she hesitates in front of their door, and listens. Nothing. After a minute, she knocks. The rapping sound is too loud, and it startles her. She steps away from the door.

A soft voice says, "Come in."

Teurith's heart flutters. The door opens before she pushes it. Yana isn't there. Two young women lounge on pillows scattered around the room. A wisp of orange smoke rises from a small golden tray on the table by the window, where she sees an ember glowing, the sweet smell that wafted into her room.

"We've been waiting for you," one of them says, and she rises from where she lay, slow and graceful.

Teurith backs towards the door, but it's closed. She doesn't remember shutting it behind her. The woman twists a strand of her long red hair in her fingers and approaches, her black eyes gazing into Teurith's.

"Where is Yana?" Teurith says, unable to look away. She blushes at the woman's beauty and nearness.

"She will arrive soon, but asked us to take care of you."

"Take care of me?"

"Come." She moves to the bed and sits, patting the empty space alongside her. "Morin, bring the brush," she says to the other woman, who stands and takes a brush out of a drawer and hands it to her.

"Morin?" Teurith says, and glances towards the door. "But—you look different."

"Yes. Our youth returns in the night. You remember me. I am Tendris. You have such beautiful hair. Let it loose so I can brush it."

Teurith hesitates. She likes her ponytail. It keeps her hair out of the way. She looks down after she pulls her hair out of the ribbon, and it hangs in her face.

"Good. Now, let me." Tendris brushes Teurith's hair with languid, caressing motions.

Teurith averts her eyes, although the attention is nice. She relaxes again. Morin opens a closet and brings out a few dresses. She tries them on. The dresses, long and gauzy, flow to the floor. Teurith has never seen such clothes. In between fittings, Morin admires her nude form in the mirror.

Teurith tries not to look.

"Beautiful, no?" Tendris says.

Teurith remains quiet.

Tendris and Morin laugh.

"Um, where do they make such clothing?" Teurith says.

"Not the dresses, silly. Morin."

Teurith looks down. "I suppose so."

"Now, you."

"What?" Teurith says, trying to stand. A dizzy spell forces her to sit.

"You try one," Tendris says, and Morin sits on the other side of Teurith.

"I don't think they'll fit me," Teurith mumbles.

"Nonsense," Morin says. "We'll help you get up and remove your clothes."

Teurith tries to move and Tendris keeps her anchored. Morin pulls at her clothes.

Teurith whimpers. "Where is Yana?"

The door opens and another woman walks into the room, veiled, with her blonde hair loose and her long slender legs visible through the diaphanous dress she wears. Before she approaches, she sets a green leather pouch stitched in gold on the floor with a soft thud.

She leans forward and takes Teurith's chin in her hand. "Well, hello, Princess Teurith."

"Just Teurith," she says, shaking. "Yana? Is it you?"

"Yes, Princess. I am beautiful, no?" Yana laughs. Morin and Tendris echo her.

The three women surround Teurith. She squirms as they tear at her clothing, then begin to touch her where she's not used to being touched. She feels warm and damp in her trousers. "Magus," she cries, halfhearted and weak.

The women grow rougher, and murmur things. Princess. Blood. Prophecy. And words she does not recognize. Teurith catches glimpses of them as she remembers how they appeared to her earlier, older, still beautiful. Then their faces morph, distorted and grinning with menace, what demons must look like. Teurith screams and wrenches herself free.

They don't stop her but cackle instead.

Teurith snaps herself aware and grabs the nearest thing she can get her hands on— the green leather gold-trimmed pouch. She grabs its leather strap and whirls it around like a flail. The women lean away and duck. With the pouch still in hand, Teurith runs out the door, screaming for Magus.

He doesn't answer.

There's no time to go back to her room. She flies into the common area and out the front door.

Then she stops short.

Magus stands in front of the inn. He smiles and extends his arms towards her.

Teurith can't move.

His eyes appear glazed over, as if he can't see her. "Teurith. All is well. Come back inside with me."

She doesn't reply, and takes a step away from him, then glances over her shoulder at the inn.

"Now, Teurith," Magus says, and walks forward. "Come." As he approaches her, his face melts away. A demented mouth with teeth sharp and askew stretches a leer across his face under fiery red eyes.

Teurith bolts. She heads north through the village of Loring and toward the Deafwood, running, running, just like in her dreams.

# IV
## *Court*
### *The Year 532*

"Y<small>OU</small> disobeyed me. This wandering has gotten out of hand," King Egad says.

Gareth glances at Egrith before saying, "We didn't think anything would happen to any of us."

"It's my fault," Egrith says. "I shouldn't have jumped the Kraken over the wall. I didn't mean for any harm to come to Dirk, or anyone."

"I have always told you. Never venture to the Barkus Wall. It is too far for you to travel alone without guards." The King addresses Dirk's father, Derrek. "Leave Dirk here for proper care. The healers will look after him."

Derrek nods.

"Gareth, you and your sister will stay within the castle walls for now. No wandering, not even in town. Gareth will continue his training with the Castle Guard, and Egrith, you will remain with Grena or at court with your sister and the other ladies. It's time, now. You are no longer a child."

Tears form in Egrith's eyes.

Argo steps forward. "My King, what can I do?"

"I should send you home to Martoldt Hall. You played as much a part in this mischief as the others. However, I believe you should continue your training here along with Gareth." The King stands.

Gareth and Egrith step back, and bow and curtsy.

"You are dismissed," the King says, and disappears through the door to his study.

In the days that follow, Egrith stays alone in her chambers. "It hasn't come for a while, but now, the dark fog has returned," she says, and gazes out the window. The town sprawls before her, with city walls and rolling green hills beyond.

Alone in her chamber with the dread feeling swirling in her gut, Egrith shakes her head. "I want to obey father. But I miss my friends." She tries the chamber door. "Not locked. And Grena's with the little ones for story time." She pulls a shawl around her shoulders. "Nobody will know where I go for now."

Down two spiral stairways, a series of hallways and through the main dining hall Egrith wends her way to the Healing Rooms. She walks through a small herd of ladies in waiting. They giggle after she passes. She looks over her shoulder and sticks her tongue out at them. "I don't care what they think."

She pushes the door open and sees Dirk in the last bed by the window. His eyes widen as she approaches, her long black hair and green dress flowing behind her. She drags a chair beside his bed and pats his hand, then sits.

"You belong at court. You're beautiful," he says.

"I hate it. They all know I'm only there because I was into mischief."

"It's best for you. You're a proper lady now."

"Father wants to have a ball to formally introduce me," she says.

"That's wonderful." Dirk holds his hand to his forehead.

"How do you feel? Still dizzy?"

"No. Not dizzy anymore, and the fever broke last night."

"What ailed you?" Egrith says.

"The healers don't say much—only that I hit my head when the horse threw me. Mostly they check on me, help me up change my nightshirt or bring food and water."

"Maybe Grena knows something," she says.

"Will you visit me when I'm home?"

"Father says no. I don't know what I'll—do without you."

Dirk lowers his head.

"I mean it. And you have to continue your reading. Tomorrow afternoon I'll bring scrolling crystals. We can look at the green one with all the maps. We'll read about the Sounding Sea, where it ends and becomes the Bask Sea to the south."

"I would like that," he says and yawns; his eyes begin to close.

Egrith returns the following day, and Dirk isn't there. "Whom to ask?" She sniffles and wipes a tear from her cheek. "Must be back at the smithy already." She rubs her stomach. "Oh, I cannot shake this darkness from me."

She stops by the Hall of Crystals on the way to her chambers. Hundreds of compartments line the walls on all sides of the room under its high ceiling, a moveable ladder at each wall. The Master of Histories sits at a desk in the middle of the room. Egrith waves at him and says, "Hello, Master Arkle."

He stands and bows. "How may I help you?" he says, and removes his monocle. His face, long and narrow, resembles a goose.

"I'm looking for a history of the Barkus Arts," she says.

"Crystals concerning magic are forbidden," he says. "Our King believes it is best not to speak on the subject."

"How about crystals concerning the Barkus Wall?"

"All off limits, I'm afraid."

"But what if they come back?"

"Who?"

"The darkest practitioners of the Barkus Arts. You know, Queen Benadras banished them to the south. How will we be prepared?" she says.

"They are far away from here, perhaps as far south as the Desert Lands."

Egrith rises and curtsies.

"You needn't worry. Go now, in peace," Master Arkle says.

"Maybe I should approach Father," she says to herself on the way to her chambers.

Grena meets her at the door when she arrives. "Where have you been? The seamstresses have been here since late morning."

"I went to see Master Arkle. Sorry I forgot, Grena."

"The Tinkers passed through last week to deliver the new silks. You need all new dresses; you're much taller now."

Egrith frowns as Grena unlaces her corset, yanking the strings out of the loops.

"You need shifts, too, as you've outgrown the ones you have," Grena says, pointing to Egrith's undergarment, which barely hangs below her knees.

"The shifts are fine. Nobody sees them under the long dresses," Egrith says.

"You need a shift to fill out the bottom of the dress so it flows," Grena says, and stops what she's doing. "Have you been to see that blacksmith's boy?"

Egrith feels heat creeping around her neck to her face.

"It's alright. I thought you'd go. His father came for him late yesterday. Better you visited him here than at the smithy."

"Is he out of the woods now?"

Grena glances at the women preparing the dresses. "We'll speak after we finish.

Now put your arms over your head and try this dress." Grena stands away to admire Egrith after lacing up the dress, which is made from a blueberry-colored silk trimmed in silver. "You should wear this to the ball. The color makes your eyes even bluer."

"That's still a long way off," Egrith says.

"You'll have a glorious time, with the dancing and new friends."

"They're all ridiculous, those girls and my sister. They just sit around all day and talk about boys and eat grapes, with occasional glances in the mirror to admire themselves."

"Now hush, Dear," Grena says.

The women leave; Grena and Egrith sit by the fireplace. "The Barkus wall is cursed, isn't it?" Egrith says.

Grena sighs. "Egrith. Your father does not want us to speak of the wall, or the magic that made it—what it is."

"That's why Dirk fell, I know it."

"After Queen Benadras ordered the construction of the wall and infused it with magic, stone masons were sent to begin, with guards from the castle watching over them. Some men developed a strange fever."

"Fever—like Dirk?"

"I can only imagine."

"What else do you know?" Egrith says.

"Before she died the queen gave an order to hunt down any remaining dark practitioners of the Barkus Arts left within the city. As the unwanted were forced to move south, they left their mark and cursed the wall."

"Do you think Dirk will recover fully?"

"Well, he has the gift of magic, and will follow his father Derrek's path in the art of weapon-making. Perhaps his gift made him susceptible to the magic lingering on the Barkus Wall, both good magic, and bad."

Egrith waits for Grena to continue.

"Only time will tell."

"If I give you something, can you send it to Dirk for me?"

Grena smiles. "Yes. I'll make sure he gets it. Now, you must dress. You'll go with Margrin and the other ladies to the Southwest Gardens for a late afternoon tea and then take dinner with your brother in the King's Chambers."

"Why do I have to wear that?" Egrith says, as Grena unfolds another long dress, heavy with thick, ornamented fabric.

"There's a chill in the air and you must look the part."

Egrith raises her arms and Grena slips the dress over her head. Deep, bluish greens, the color of hemlock trees trimmed with gold, complement Egrith's complexion and dark hair. She heaves a sigh.

"Hold still," Grena says, as she laces and tightens the corset again.

"I don't like them. And Dirk was right about Margrin."

"What has your sister done now?"

"She's a snoot and she does smell."

Grena laughs. "Some of the younger ladies spend too much time in the perfumed baths. You'll find a place for yourself in their midst. Be patient. The night of the ball will be a treasured time for you. *Not long youth lasteth, and old age hasteth. Now is best leisure, to take our pleasure.*" Grena continues singing the madrigal tune until Egrith is dressed, then steps back to admire her. "There. See? You will be the most beautiful."

"That's no comfort," Egrith says.

"Now, now. Go, Egrith. You may surprise yourself and enjoy it."

Egrith slips into her shoes and tries to smile.

The Southwest Gardens are on the opposite side of the castle from Egrith's chambers and it takes her a while to get there. She arrives and opens the door where the afternoon sun bathes the courtyard in its light. Benches stand among trees and bushes; flowers decorate the spaces in between with color. Other young women sit or stand talking in small groups. They turn to Egrith and curtsy as she approaches. Margrin leads her group of four to Egrith.

"It's nice of you to join us," Margrin says. "Your dress is lovely, a far cry from the breeches you usually wear." She smiles, takes a sip from her teacup and moves aside with the others.

Egrith does not smile. "Thank you. I can't very well go riding warhorses in this thing," she says with a glance down at her dress. She excuses herself.

In a corner of the garden where the castle wall is higher, a girl sits by herself holding a scrolling crystal. Egrith takes two cups of tea from the serving woman and walks over to the girl, who looks up and squints.

"Hello. Would you like a cup of tea?" Egrith says.

"Oh, thank you." The girl sips from the cup and smiles.

"You don't seem too comfortable over her alone."

"I know. I just—like it here. Too crowded over there," she says with a look at Margrin and the others.

Egrith shakes her head. "Don't worry. They don't have anything better to do than needle people for not being exactly like they are. What's your name?"

"My name is Loren. And you're Princess Egrith."

"I'm surprised we haven't met. I thought I knew everyone."

"I'm sick a lot. I usually stay with my mother in her room."

"I haven't even seen you in the Hall of Crystals," Egrith says.

"Mother brings me scrolling crystals to read. Now that I'm feeling stronger she says I must get out more—and spend time with the other ladies." Loren frowns.

"I know they can be unkind."

"No, they simply ignore me. That's no fun either." She pauses, turns away and sneezes.

"Blessings for your health," Egrith says.

"Thank you."

"What are you reading?"

Loren hands Egrith the scrolling crystal.

Egrith smiles and reads the title aloud. "A History of Royal Lineage from the Beginning of Time."

"You're descended from Queen Benadras."

"Yes. She decreed the scribes to record the new time from the building of the Barkus Wall. We know there's a lot of history before that. They say each land of the world has its own history and measurement of time."

"I would love to know more. You know so much," Loren says.

"Well, I read constantly, even apart from lessons with Master Arkle."

"Master Arkle is a dear man. He's courting mother."

"Another pronouncement my father made. Widows may remarry if they choose. I'm happy for you and your mother. Master Arkle is sweet."

They remain quiet for a few minutes as the sun begins to set.

"Loren. What do you know about the Barkus Wall?"

Loren sits up straighter. "I know there are crystals that are now forbidden to us."

Egrith lowers her voice. "Do you have access to the keys for the Hall of Crystals?"

"Master Arkle keeps them clipped to his belt."

"Oh," Egrith says.

"I can't get them for you. I would be in deep trouble," Loren says.

"I just want to have a look at the forbidden crystals when no one's around."

"Master Arkle doesn't say much, but he told mother he doesn't approve."

"Approve of what?"

"Of—I shouldn't say this to you—of the King's desire to keep certain histories hidden."

"That's our fault," Egrith says. "We rode to the Barkus Wall and Dirk fell off his horse and caught a fever."

"That's awful." Loren whispers. "Maybe you shouldn't be so inquisitive. But—"

"What?"

"There might be a hidden room where more crystals are stored."

"I wonder where that could be? If they keep them hidden we'll never understand anything. What if Dirk doesn't get better?"

Margrin approaches with her friends. "What are you two talking about?"

Loren stays quiet.

Egrith stands. "Oh, we're just having a look at Loren's crystal. She's very smart, you know."

"Too much attention to reading. That's why she doesn't have companions," Margrin says. The other young ladies giggle.

Egrith helps Loren stand and takes her arm. "Well, she does now." Egrith and Loren walk past Margrin and her entourage.

They curtsy and stand aside.

"Thank you," Loren says as they leave the garden. "I knew once they finally spoke to me it wouldn't be nice."

"They don't have much imagination and won't bother you. Let's stick together," Egrith says.

"I hope you won't go too far with your crystal hunting."

"Don't worry. I won't. But I might have a look at a map of the castle," Egrith says.

"For hidden rooms?"

"Some of the older maps might show something. The crystals may be kept in one of those rooms."

# V

## *The Stone*
### *The Year 548*

Teurith races into the Deafwood, and she begins to remember the dreams—her tattered tunic, the sticky, dampness of her leggings, running, running without rest. The memory of her dreams, which she could not recall earlier, flood through her, happening once again now as she flees. And Magus, their dear friend, changed—just like those women.

She can't go home. That's the first place they'll look. For a moment, she thinks of what she left behind in her room at the inn—the scrolling crystals Father gave her. He always said the ability to read is a gift. He taught her how.

In the thick of trees, she can't see a path and slows her pace, the weight of the leather pouch she stole bouncing against her side as she flees. She's south of the clearing where she saw the vision of the blond witch. That must have been real as well.

*It was all real.*

Teurith sweats, and as the wind kicks up, she shivers. But she keeps moving. Eventually, she reaches a path and continues south through the forest. Branches from bushes of laurel brush her as she runs; the path becomes narrower. A pain in her side forces her to slow down, and she stops where the laurel is thicker, where she might rest. Teurith curls up under the branches of a laurel bush, and holds the pouch to her breast. For now, the dark will protect her.

Teurith awakens, startled by the sound of her own whimpering. In the cold dampness of early morning fog, she remembers the pouch and shifts her position on the ground so she can sit up. She opens it, reaches in, and feels the coarse heaviness of what can only be a lump of rock. The stone warms in her hand, then feels more like glass, expanding similar to the way a scrolling crystal does. Teurith lets it fall to the ground where it dims and returns to its rock-like appearance. She shoves it in the pouch where it belongs.

Morning light brightens as she walks the path, still heading south. She recognizes landmarks of the Deafwood and should reach the meadow soon. The fog clears. She knows where she is, not where she's going. Blueberries grow along the path. There aren't many. She pulls them from the bushes and eats what she can. She'll need water soon, too, and she's still an hour north of the stream.

She thinks of Father. If she travels along the road at night, she can make it to Riverton in a few days. The meadow is near. Cautious, she edges along the trees. There isn't much cover in the meadow—tall grass, a few straggly bushes and some rock formations. She crouches and makes slow progress. Voices carry over the clearing, coming from the northeast. Teurith's heart pounds and she flattens on her stomach in the tall grass.

"Teurith!" someone calls, followed by other masculine voices calling her name.

She doesn't hear any feminine voices.

A high, moss-covered rock stands a few paces away. Teurith moves faster until she reaches it. She still hears voices. In the shadow of the rock, she peeks around and sees Knut, the man she remembers from the inn who travels with the three witch-women.

Teurith watches him sniff at the air. She shudders.

He stops sniffing, turns her direction, and approaches the rock where Teurith hides, his steps slow and deliberate.

If she runs, he'll see her. She presses herself to the side of the rock in its shade. Her body shakes and her teeth chatter. She doesn't know where Knut is. Fear grips her heart.

"Teurith!"

She recognizes Magus' deep voice. For a moment, she wants to run to him. Maybe he is himself now. Teurith remains quiet and stays where she is.

"Knut," Magus' voice calls. "I think we found something."

The sound of Knut's footsteps receding steadies her nerves. As Magus calls her name again she crawls along the ground, and continues toward the forest. After crouching along for quite a while, she finally reaches the south side of the meadow, and leaves the voices behind.

Teurith stands and stretches. In the woods, she feels protected. She finds another path and heads southward through the trees. Like she thought, she runs into the stream after an hour. She kneels and splashes her face, then drinks from the cold, clear water.

"Who are you?" a voice says.

Teurith falls on her bottom, her legs kicking out in front of her. She scrambles and tries to turn around to where she heard the voice. A little boy steps from behind a tree and stares at her with his hands on his hips.

"Who are you?" he says again.

"Nobody. I'm passing through," Teurith says, collects herself and rises. She's taller than he is but backs away from him.

"Where do you come from?"

"Where do *you* come from?" she replies, brushing her leggings off.

"You first," he says. His knickers are made from a shiny material, orange with a black belt holding them up. His shirt is yellow and billowy, tucked in at the waist.

"I don't have time for games. I'm tired and hungry and I need to get to my father."

"Where's he?"

"Too many questions," she says and starts walking south again.

"Wait!"

Teurith turns and faces him. "What are you doing here by yourself, anyway?"

"I'm lost," he says. "And you stink."

Teurith looks down at her pants. They're damp and sticky. She pulls her pant leg away from her skin at the thigh. "Are your people in the forest?"

"They're by the road at the mountains."

"North of here or south?"

He cocks his head to one side, turns and points into the woods.

"That's not helpful," Teurith says. "C'mon. We can head west until we run into the road, then we can turn south." The boy will slow her down. His people may have food for her, though, and she begins walking.

"What's your name?" he says.

Teurith hesitates. "Not your business."

"I'm Nathal. My Poppa died but the Marmas, and maybe even The Quenn, will reward you for finding me."

"I didn't find you. You snuck up on me," she says.

"And they'll give you food and you can stay with us." He continues to chatter about his family. "My uncles are tall and strong. They ride ahead sometimes to scout. My Marma works at the looms with the other Marmas."

Teurith walks faster.

"Hey, wait," he says.

"You talk too much."

"What's in the bag?"

"Not your business."

They finally come to the road that winds through the foothills of the mountains. The sun's still high and they stay along the woods as they walk south. Teurith often looks over her shoulder.

"What's wrong?" Nathal says.

"Nothing." She's weak, and slows her pace until the ground flattens and becomes more even. After another half an hour, Teurith smells the smoke of campfires. She stops.

"We found them," Nathal says, takes her hand and pulls her forward.

They come to a large caravan of wagons. People dressed like Nathal in bright-colored clothing mill about tents and among campfires. Nathal runs and disappears into one of the wagons. He comes out right away, leading a woman in a green dress by the hand. She is of medium height and her black, shiny hair flows to the middle of her back.

The woman squints her dark brown eyes at Teurith as Nathal chatters. "...and she found me and brought me back. Don't know her name. She stinks like dead possum and she's quiet but she—"

"Hush, Natty." The woman approaches Teurith. "Welcome. Thank you for bringing Nathal to us. Natty, go and gather some twigs. And don't wander away."

Nathal obeys and moves to the edge of the woods with a final glance over his shoulder at Teurith.

"Are you hungry?" the woman says.

"Yes."

The woman tries to take Teurith's hand and she pulls away.

"I am Jesmane." She looks at Teurith's clothing, which is dirty and torn, her eyes lingering on her leggings. "Do you know about the blooding?"

Teurith steps back, swallows and says, "Blooding?"

"You have the blood."

"I don't—know what that means." Before she can stop herself, she thinks of the women at the inn, the way their hands moved over her, and where they touched her, vaguely aware of the pain she feels from their prodding. She winces.

"Come with me."

Teurith follows the woman into one of the wagons where two other women sit at a loom. The wagon is cramped but the women make room for Jesmane and Teurith.

"This is Malya," Jesmane says, gesturing to a plump woman who smiles and continues weaving, "and this is Kala." Kala stands and approaches. Kala's hair is also long and dark. The pale blue of her dress makes her brown skin stand out, striking in the afternoon light.

"Tell us your name," Kala says.

"I—I can't."

"You have to change your clothing," Jesmane says.

Teurith trembles and her teeth chatter again.

"Kala, draw water for her in the bathing tent," Jesmane says and turns to Teurith. "Please, don't be afraid. We'll find you something to wear and wait for you to finish."

In a tent at the edge of the caravan, Teurith stands for a while, listening. She pulls the flaps aside, peeks out, and doesn't see anyone. Then she slowly peels her clothes off, shivering. She notices dark red stains on her leggings and underthings. *Blood.* The witch-women from the inn must have hurt her badly to make her bleed so much.

Teurith lowers herself into the tub. The water is warmer than she thought it would be, and she begins to relax, her aching body soothed. She soaps layers of grime off her feet and arms. Then she leans back and soaks. After a while she hears someone speak to her from outside, Jesmane, she thinks.

"How are you doing?"

"A bit better," Teurith says.

"Supper is almost ready. Here are clothes and cloths for the blooding. Take the cloths and fit them into your undergarments."

*Blooding?*

"Thank you."

*Yes, she's bleeding, but why?*

Teurith dries herself and sees the clothes. Undergarments and a dark red dress sit folded neatly by the entrance to the tent. To her horror, she realizes she's still bleeding and it doesn't stop. Along with the dress there are some soft cloths of different colors, like Jesmane said. She places one in the pantaloons and puts them on. The chemise is long and she pulls it over her head, and then the dress, which is fitted to her form. Her hair is wet but clean.

On a stool, she sees the green leather pouch with the rock in it sitting where she left it. She's sighs her relief, realizing she almost forgot about it. She grabs the pouch and pushes the tent flaps aside, walks through and finds Jesmane, Kala and Malya waiting outside. They murmur among themselves and Teurith steps back.

"You look beautiful," Kala says, and the other women smile.

Teurith blushes.

"It's time for supper," Jesmane says and turns toward the wagons.

Teurith follows the women. Men sit on the backs of wagons drinking from flagons and eating meat with their hands, while children scurry from one tent or wagon to another, and other women bustle around the fires doling out supper. Older children, more of Teurith's age, sit in groups with occasional glances at her.

As Teurith eats, she marvels at the way they're all dressed alike, the brilliant colors of fabrics she's never seen before. The curtained windows of the wagons even have colored cloth like their clothing.

Jesmane sits on the edge of a wagon next to Teurith. "Do you enjoy the dinner?"

"Yes." Teurith doesn't know what to say. They're kind to her but she has to get moving and find Father.

"The sun will set soon. We go to the smoking tent for the evening after supper. You come with us."

Then something occurs to Teurith, and she says, "You're the Tinker-folk, aren't you?"

Jesmane smiles. "Ah, yes. Tinkers. And it is said we steal children from their beds at night and then sell them in the cities."

"But, you don't." Teurith pauses. "Do you?"

Jesmane laughs. "No. We spend our winters in the far south, where we prepare the looms for spinning silk. Then we travel way north to sell our wares. By the season of the rains we go to Riverton and then south again for winter."

"You make this clothing?"

"Yes. We spin the silk and our dyers mix the colors, then our seamstresses fashion patterns and stitch the clothing together. Come, now."

Teurith follows Jesmane and the others to a large tent, the pinnacle of it high enough for a tall man to stand straight. There are already several women there, girls not much older than she, and much older women, smoking long, spindly pipes, not like the short, brown thick one Father has, but decorated with carvings on the white bowls. Smoke curls upwards as she wades through the women.

Jesmane leads Teurith to a stool in the corner. She listens to the women talk for a while. Then all eyes turn towards her. Teurith sits straighter, wondering what's happening. Then Jesmane speaks.

"You are no longer a child. Your blooding will happen every month for many years. Do not be afraid, or ashamed of it. Keep the cloths and clothing you were given. A gift from us for bringing Natty back safely."

"I don't understand. You mean, this—this bleeding is natural?"

"Yes. It signifies you are into womanhood, and may bear children when you wish."

Teurith tries to understand. But she thinks of the witches at the inn, probably looking for her, and what she stole from them. She shivers.

"Is there something else?" Jesmane says, and her eyes turn to the green pouch Teurith holds at her side.

Teurith hugs the pouch to her chest, and tenses up, her eyes darting around for a way out.

"Don't be afraid," the women murmur, and they gather around her.

Teurith doesn't feel threatened. Cautious and slow, she pulls the rock from the pouch, holds it up in the lantern light, and it begins to glow. She imagines she also feels it pulsate in her hands, and she almost drops it, then she puts it away.

"Careful, girl," one of the older women says.

"What is it?" Teurith says.

The women back away from her and form a circle.

"It is said the stone artifact will fall into good hands before the treacherous ones can make ill use of it. If you are the chosen one, you're not safe here, or anywhere."

"I do have to leave and find Father."

Teurith sits quietly, hugging the pouch to her chest while the women talk amongst themselves, stealing an occasional glance at her.

Jesmane returns, followed by the other women. "We must commune and make a decision as to what to do with you. You must not leave.

# VI

## *Conversations*
### *The Year 532*

"MOTHER told me I can go with you. I just hope it's not cold in there," Loren says.

"At least we'll be together," Egrith says.

They make their way to the lowest floor of the castle, above the caverns. When they reach the northeast corner, they see guards standing outside the women's entrance. As they approach, the guards stand aside and let them pass.

"Why are there guards?" Loren says.

"They weren't needed until the sons of a visiting lord made mischief and crept around, probably hoping to see the women bathing. It turned out they saw Grandmama and her two friends wading in the shallows instead."

"What happened?"

Egrith laughs. "Grandmama's friends screamed and startled the boys, and she threatened to give them fleas then they ran away."

"Your Grandmama Nora?"

"Yes. Mother's mother. She had the gifts of seeing and spell-casting—and she loved to laugh—always laughed when she told that story— 'And they fled from our old, sagging nakedness and threats of fleas.'" Egrith laughs. Then she sighs and turns away, shielding her eyes.

"Egrith?"

"I'm sorry. Speaking of Grandmama Nora makes me think of my—" She swallows and bites her lip. "—my mother."

"I've heard of your mother's beauty and kindness," Loren says, keeping her voice soft.

Egrith shivers and shakes her head, then smiles. "It actually is a bit chilly in here." She leads Loren to a room with a low ceiling and arches connecting stone columns. Steam rises from the water where women stand and talk in small groups.

Loren whispers, "I thought they'd, you know, have something for us to wear."

"The shifts for bathing are hanging on that wall," Egrith says, pointing. "Some ladies choose to go in without. Let's dress in here where it's warmer." She grabs two shifts and leads Loren into the steaming chamber.

Loren sits on one of the benches. "This heat is delicious. How is it so warm?"

"Natural hot springs under this part of the castle warm the stones under the benches. The water travels through a series of pipes and becomes cooler before it reaches the baths. But in the steaming chamber, there's a hot spring directly under the stones." Egrith peeks out the door. "Oh, glunk."

"What is it?" Loren says.

"My stupid sister and her equally stupid friends are here."

Loren stays quiet.

"Let's leave after they're in the water."

They put their dresses on again, and sneak among the shadows along the wall. As they approach the arched doorway by the guards they hear someone shout after them.

"Father's looking for you. You had better hurry."

"Ugh." Egrith stomps her foot. "Margrin knows everything. She doesn't care about me one snippet and only gets nosy about what I'm doing when she wants to have something to gossip to her friends about."

"Maybe she's bored," Loren says. "I'm sure she must care for you."

"She resents me." Egrith sniffles.

"Why?"

"Because mother died when she gave birth to me." Egrith wipes her eyes. "I am sorry. I've been a mess for two years now."

"You're not a mess, really," Loren says.

"Yes. I am. Ever since the blooding, I cry and get irritated, and I experience things with such passion."

"I know that's hard, especially with the cramping and worry of it. But, isn't feeling deeply a gift?"

Egrith pauses. "I never thought of it that way. If it is a gift, it's a curse, too."

They follow the hallways until they reach the stairs to the Great Dining Hall, where long oak tables fill the room and tapestries depicting historical events stretch over the stone walls. Egrith looks toward the top of the stairway. "Gareth," she shouts and begins climbing. "Wait for us."

Gareth turns at the sound of her voice, and smiles. "Father—"

"I know, I know. He wants to see me."

They reach the top of the stairs and Loren stands behind Egrith, who takes her hand and pulls her forward. "And this is my friend Loren."

Gareth bows. "I am charmed."

Loren curtsies, lowering her head so her blush won't show.

"Will I see you at Egrith's ball?" he says.

Loren smooths her dress. "If mother says I may."

"Oh, you'll have an invitation and she won't be able to deny you the pleasure," Egrith says.

On the opposite end of the hall, Argo takes the stairs down by twos and starts walking across to the others. Egrith laughs at something, and he stops short, then studies one of the tapestries depicting a warrior with a flaming sword.

Gareth calls to him. "Argo. You're just in time to meet Loren."

Argo walks to them. "Hello," he says with a bow for Loren; he turns his eyes to Egrith.

"Oh, hello. Can I talk with you a moment?" Egrith says, taking Argo's arm.

Argo lets her drag him to a corner of the hall, where he stands stiff and quiet.

She keeps her voice low. "Have you seen Dirk?"

"I have," he says, as his face darkens.

"What's wrong, isn't he better?"

"Much."

"Phew. I've been so worried. Why the angry face? Are you mad?" she says.

"No." He looks away.

Egrith taps him on the shoulder. "Will you please give him some things for me? Grena says she won't because crystals mustn't leave the castle. But he has to keep up with his reading and I can't help him anymore."

"What's so important about reading, anyway?" Argo says.

"Well, it's a skill everyone should have, not just mages and scholars—and the wealthy. I think all people should be able to learn the histories and even study magic if they want—"

"You're in love with him."

"No, it's not that. I just miss him, and—"

"Yes. You are," he says.

Egrith stays quiet for a moment, and lowers her voice. "And what if I am. What do you care?"

"I don't. I don't care at all. You're a spoiled child and I don't even like you."

Egrith's lip trembles and she runs past Gareth and Loren to the stairs.

Argo watches as she descends.

Gareth strides to Argo. "What did you say to my sister?"

"Nothing."

"You upset her. She's sad enough, and cries all of the time. You shouldn't make her cry, too."

"I'm sorry. I didn't know."

"Stay away from her," Gareth says, and leaves.

Argo glances at Loren briefly before climbing the stairs himself.

Egrith runs, although tears blind her. She slows down as she approaches her father's chambers, and she steels her nerves, then knocks.

Her father's steward answers the door and stands aside to let her pass. "The Princess Egrith."

King Egad quickens his step toward his daughter when he sees her tear-streaked face. "Dearest, what troubles you?" He takes her in his arms as she sobs.

"Oh, father, I'm sorry I took the Kraken and I'm sorry I dragged Gareth and Argo into it, and I'm sorry about Dirk—"

"Hush, Child. I've been looking into the situation. Derrek said Dirk feels more himself, and continues with his metalworking. He will be an important blacksmith one day, as he was born with the gift his father has."

Egrith sniffles. "He will learn to make magical weapons, as his father does?"

"Yes, Egrith. And I know he's your friend, and you haven't many. But I like this young Loren. It is good for you to have an ally. I will visit her mother and ask that she attend the ball myself."

"What about—Dirk?"

"He certainly cannot attend your coming-of-age celebration. However, I have thought on it. You may visit with him, and only if you remain within the walls of the city. No tramping around the countryside."

"Father, thank you." She curtsies and then hugs him.

The sun is still high. Egrith hurries to her chamber and grabs her cloak. She pauses, then opens the wardrobe door, and bends to rifle through the pile in the back of it. In the midst of her riding clothes and extra blankets, she finds the bundle. She unwraps it, careful not to drop one of the crystals. She chooses the first crystal she finds, the blue one with histories she read with Dirk the day she jumped the Barkus Wall, and places it in her knapsack.

She hurries through the castle to the main gate, her heart aflutter with anticipation.

She passes the market where venders stand by their wagons selling vegetables from the recent harvest—squash, apples, husks of corn and pumpkins, and hunters peddle their dried meats and furs. She stops to examine a wrap made of silver fox fur and smiles as she imagines Loren warmed by soft fur around her neck. Her stomach churns with anticipation; she continues walking towards the smithy.

She turns the last corner and sees Dirk sitting on a bench outside. He smokes a pipe, coughing out smoke in short bursts.

"Yoo-hoo," Egrith sings from around the corner.

Dirk stands, and scratches his head. "It can't be."

Egrith's laughter snaps Dirk alert. She runs to him.

They embrace and he lets go first, then steps back with a half-smile.

"Are you finished for the day?" she says.

"Just about. Trying out a present from Father," he says, reddens, and taps the bowl of the pipe against the bench. "Although I'm not very good at it yet."

"It smells good, kind of like the woodstove in Grena's rooms." She hesitates. "Dirk?"

"What?"

"I'm sorry I missed your name day. But I have something for you, too."

"I don't need a gift. I'm just glad you came by," he says.

"Any way your father will let you clean up and come with me for a while?"

"Think so. Come in while I ask."

Egrith shakes her head. "I'll wait here, thank you."

"Don't worry. He isn't angry."

"Alright," she says, and follows Dirk into the smithy.

The forge, in the center of the room, glows and crackles. Dirk's father Derrek leans over a table, about to set a pale blue crystal stone onto the hilt of a sword. Egrith and Dirk, careful not to disrupt, hear him murmur short phrases in the ancient tongue while he sets the stone in place. The crystal shines a shade of dark blue light that fills the room, and then sinks into the metal, returning to its pale color.

Derrek exhales slowly and sits on a bench.

Dirk approaches and says, "Father?"

Derrek shifts his position and faces his son. "Are you finished for the day?" He smiles at Egrith. "Hello, Child. It is good to have you with us once again."

Egrith curtsies. "Thank you, Sir. I can wait while Dirk finishes, but may I walk with him for a while after?"

"Why don't you go now? I'll clean up. Alright with you, Dirk?"

"Yes, Father. We won't be late."

"Before the sun sets, Dirk."

"I'll be back by then."

Egrith takes Dirk's hand and leads him out the door. They stroll down the lane until they reach the city wall.

"Which way?" he says.

"There's that big grove of trees toward the southwestern corner. It'll take us a few minutes but it'll be quiet there. Everyone's at market today."

They walk in silence broken by occasional birdsong and the sound of squirrels jumping from branch to branch in the trees nearby. The brush thickens and the trees are taller as they near the corner of the city walls. Egrith quickens her pace as they move through the woods.

"Gods, Egrith, what's the rush?" Dirk says.

"I don't want to waste any of this time," she says, and stops when she hears water running. "I forgot about the stream. Let's sit here." She takes the small coverlet from her knapsack and spreads it on the ground next to the water. She frowns at Dirk, who stands a few paces away. "Well, c'mon, silly."

His face turns ashen, but he sits by her side. "Uh…" he begins, then closes his mouth.

"What is it?"

"Um…what's this gift you have for me?"

Egrith reaches for her knapsack. "Let me show you." She smiles at him and removes the bundle. "Close your eyes and hold out your hands."

"Alright." He obeys.

"Keep them closed and take a guess," she says.

Dirk keeps his arms stretched toward Egrith and soon feels the cool smoothness of a crystal in his hands. "Oh, no, more reading," he groans, but smiles and opens his eyes.

Egrith laughs, and then becomes quiet, watching Dirk for a moment as he turns the crystal tablet over in his hands.

"That was always my favorite thing—reading with you." He gazes at the stream.

Egrith blushes before he sees her. "Well, let's get started."

They sit side-by-side and hold the crystal between them. They feel it grow warm. It expands and words materialize, scrolling as Dirk begins to read. "The Battle of the Mage-Warriors rag-guh-ed—"

"Raged," Egrith says.

"Raged…as Bartolus—we read about him in the summer months—and his flaming sword slice through the frontline of the Queen's army."

"Wonderful, Dirk. Keep going."

"The Royal Cavalry…char-char-charges from the east and west sides and surround Bartolus. He stands surrounded by a…battle-uh-bat-tali-on—"

"Battalion."

"—of warriors protecting him with a shield wall. The shields glow with flame and ward off the approach of the Queen's horses. Many horses fall, throwing their riders to the ground where they lay, vulnerable to fire and weapon. Phew. Can we take a break?"

"But I'm enjoying this," she says, and laughs.

Dirk smiles.

"What has you amused?"

"Nothing—you—not you. I'm not amused by you at all—I mean—you're—engaging—and everything—but I'm not laughing at you," Dirk says. "I just like the sound of your laughter. Like bunches of tiny bells tinkling all at once."

"You're sweet," Egrith says, then stays quiet until Dirk looks away again. "I've missed you very much."

He says nothing, and avoids her eyes.

"I do have a new friend, a distant cousin who was sickly as a child. Now she's stronger and we spend time together."

"I like that you have a new friend. You deserve that—and more," Dirk says to the stream.

"But I miss being with you," she says. "Don't you miss me, too?"

He starts to turn his head to the water again and Egrith stops him with her hand on his arm. He pulls away.

"Let me see you, your eyes. Please. I do not know your thoughts."

Dirk mumbles under his breath.

"What? Am I disgusting?" Egrith says, and stands.

"No, no, please don't talk. Let's read again," he says, as he rises from where he's sitting and meets her gaze. "Here." He stoops and picks up the crystal tablet. "We can—" He sees Egrith's tears and takes her in his arms.

She sobs.

"There, there. I am clumsy. I never say the right thing."

She cries harder, and gasps, "It's not—not what you say or don't say. It's like we're puppies together, busy chasing rabbits and running through the woods."

"You don't want me to talk?" Dirk releases her and takes a cloth out of his pocket. He wipes tears from her cheeks, her chin, her eyes.

For a moment, they stay still.

Then, Egrith tries to look away.

He stops her, cups her chin in his hand, turns her face towards his, and kisses her. She doesn't resist.

Daylight fades and their lips finally part.

In the dusky evening light, they walk close together up Smithy Lane. Then Egrith drops Dirk's hand and hurries away. Before she turns the corner, she watches Dirk walk through the door, then remembers she forgot to give him the crystals. As she approaches their home she smells the scent of his father's pipe wafting out the window. She's about to knock on the door when she hears them talking. She peeps through the window.

"You'll never see her again if the King becomes aware of your involvement," Derrek says, smoke rising above him.

Dirk sits on the bench across from his father. "I know."

"I'm not angry, my Son. Your mother and I were young as well. But your heart will break if you continue."

The candle flickers, and Dirk glances over his shoulder, then at his father, and stands. "It already has."

Egrith steps back from the window and wipes fresh tears from her eyes. "Poor Dirk," she whispers. "We might both be in trouble before long." She sighs and makes her way home.

# VII
## *Flight*
### *The Year 548*

TEURITH waits. The elder women haven't emerged from the tent. They will decide her fate, and she isn't afraid. She likes them, and the way they explained the blooding to her, as if she were one of their own. Long into the evening she sits, then finally leans against a tree and sleeps.

She awakens to a gentle grip on her shoulder.

"Come, Teurith," Jesmane says.

Teurith follows Jesmane into the tent, where a group of women rise from their pillows.

Jesmane faces Teurith, and says, "We have decided."

The crowd parts for another woman, and she shuffles forward. Her wooden staff, carved with delicate flowers below a crystal at the top, thumps on the ground. She nods at Teurith, and the lines etched into her ancient face become more visible as she smiles. "I am The Quenn. I have seen much in my long life."

*The Quenn?*

"Elder Woman of this tribe." She raises her staff and the crystal on it glows, filling the room with an orangey light. "And I see you."

*Me?*

"Yes, dear Child."

Teurith realizes she hasn't opened her mouth to speak, and her eyes widen.

"Yes. I can hear your thoughts. You must go, and take the stone with you, as you are meant to have it."

*What do you mean?*

"The stone is forged with your blood."

*Blood?*

"More will be made known to you," The Quenn says.

Teurith tries to speak, but can't.

"It is time, young Teurith. You must go. But not alone."

*Who will go with me?*

The Quenn smiles and moves away, disappearing into the throng of elder women, the glow from her staff fading.

Jesmane approaches Teurith. "You must rest."

Teurith follows Jesmane to a small tent in the middle of the encampment.

"You have only a few hours. I will wake you before dawn," Jesmane says.

Teurith tries to recall everything that happened in the tent with the elder women. She yawns and her eyes droop; sleep comes before she can remember what The Quenn said.

*The light in the room weakens. Teurith sees her reflection in the mirror, her long hair flowing around her face. A jeweled necklace the color of her blue eyes circles her neck until she unclasps it and lets it fall, where it clinks on the floor; the sound startles her. She feels the weight of the blue velvet dress she wears, burdensome on her frame, and pulls at its laces to free herself. But she doesn't have the strength. She gazes at the reflection again, her tear-streaked face and heavy, listless eyes pitiful in the dimness.*

*But Teurith never had a dress like that, and she doesn't recognize her surroundings. An eerie green light floods the room and three hooded figures appear behind her in the mirror's refection. She turns around. The tallest lowers its hood, revealing a face twisted with menace in the dull light, auburn hair pulled back from her face and black eyes. The other two remain hooded.*

*"You. Where is it?" the black-eyed woman says, pointing at Teurith, thick golden rings glittering on her fingers.*

*"Where is what?" Teurith says, trembling.*

*"The stone."*

*"Which stone?"*

*"You know," the woman says, and the other two reveal their faces, demon faces, hideous to behold.*

*They step forward.*

Teurith's heart thumps as the room shifts and darkness swallows the scene. She wakes up, shaky and soaked with sweat. She remembers them—the women from the inn. And her reflection in the mirror looked like her, but wasn't.

Jesmane opens the tent flap and enters with garments draped over her arm. "Here is a dress suitable for traveling and a cloak to ward off the cold. You must dress quickly."

Teurith changes and steps outside, where Jesmane stands with a boy not much older than she. He is lean and tall, and wears dark green clothing, the color of evergreen trees. Thick, black curls frame his face; his dark, almond-shaped eyes meet hers.

"Djáraad will travel with you. He is a skilled hunter, and able to defend you if necessary," Jesmane says.

He nods.

Teurith notices the bow and quiver of arrows hanging on his shoulder, and an array of knives in their scabbards line his belt.

Jesmane turns to Teurith, and drapes the dark cloak around her shoulders. "Here is your pouch. Protect it. Stay off the roadways. Our thoughts are ever with you."

Teurith takes the pouch, a sack with provisions of food—and a searing crystal.

Jesmane embraces Djáraad, then Teurith.

"Let's get moving," Djáraad says.

"Wait," Teurith says. "They're looking for me. There was this man with a sword…" She pauses.

"We are aware of these things," Jesmane says. "It is more important for you to remain safe. Go, now."

They leave in the quiet, heavy mist of early morning, and walk in silence for the first hour. The sky brightens as they encounter less familiar terrain. At times the paths narrow and they must push branches aside so they can pass through. After another few hours, a rustling sound startles them and they stop. A deer crosses the path ahead. They watch as it leaps into the brush and disappears. The sun rises higher and they come to a stream.

"We rest here," Djáraad says and sits on a rock.

Teurith takes two apples from the sack and gives one to him. He nods and crunches into it. When Teurith finishes hers, she tosses the core into the stream.

"No," Djáraad says. He rises and crosses the water, hopping from stone to stone. He stoops to pick up the apple core. "They'll know we've been here if they find this." He buries the cores at the other side of the stream. Then Teurith crosses, hiking her skirts so they won't get wet.

Djáraad waits for her and glances around. "You'd better fill your water pouch," he says.

"Alright," she says, and bends to let the water seep into the flask.

"We'll follow the stream south. That'll eventually take us to Lake Ührr. Then we move into the forest again and stop for the day."

"How long until we reach the King's Road?" Teurith says.

"Two or three days, but after tomorrow we travel only at night. And there won't be much cover near the road."

They walk for hours until the trees become sparse. The banks finally widen and they come to the lake, where the stream ends and flows into it. Geese fly overhead, honking.

"Shhh." Djáraad takes his bow and removes an arrow. He nocks it and raises the bow, slow and steady.

Teurith stays still.

The arrow whizzes past Teurith and fells a rabbit on the edge of a clearing.

"We should not have a fire." Djáraad picks up the rabbit, ties its feet together, then slings it over his shoulder. "Jesmane gave us the searing crystal, the only one of its kind in our tribe."

They move along the northern edge of the lake until they hear the falls roaring in the distance. The woods thicken and the moon rises above the tree line, casting its reflection on the water in the last minutes of daylight.

"Now. Into the trees for the night. We need a hot meal and sleep," Djáraad says.

"What direction tomorrow? Along the river?"

"First we have to get down to it."

"What does that mean?"

Djáraad gazes across Lake Ührr then squints to see better. "Let's take cover first, and I'll explain."

Under tall evergreens the forest is quiet. Pine needles and leaves carpet the forest floor, and they get settled. Djáraad places his bow and arrow on the ground close by, hangs the rabbit from a low tree branch and skins it.

"We need to block the light from the crystal as much as we can—it'll flash when we sear the rabbit," he says and opens the sack, then removes a garnet-colored stone from it.

"How do we do that?" Teurith says.

"Take your cloak off, stretch it out and hold it up. That's all."

Teurith sheds her cloak and stands with it to shield the light. "Hurry. My arms ache."

Djáraad holds the crystal in his hands and it glows a fiery red. He presses the tip of it to the rabbit and jumps back; the rabbit glows and a brief flash brightens the forest as the rabbit ignites. They smell the aroma of cooked meat and smoke rises from the skinned carcass.

"That was fast," Teurith says, lowering her arms. She wraps her cloak around her shoulders and sees Djáraad, who stares into the woods.

"What's wrong?" she says.

He raises his hand to silence her and pulls a knife from his boot.

"What?" she says.

"Keep your voice down. I thought I heard something."

"Well, I have to go away for a few minutes."

"You can't go alone."

"Yes, I can." Teurith steps into the thick of trees before Djáraad can stop her.

She finds a denser group of bushes and moves into them. After she finishes she places a fresh cloth in her undergarments, then pulls them up and smooths her dress. They'll have to burn the cloths so theit scent won't alert anything to their presence—

A twig snaps.

Teurith whirls around.

She sees nothing in the darkness and starts to call for Djáraad when a hand clamps her mouth shut. As she struggles to get away she hears a grunt in her ear. Her assailant removes his hand and faces her. She doesn't move, doesn't make a sound. He twists one of her arms, and points to the green and gold pouch with his other hand.

Teurith sees Knut and shakes her head no.

Knut pushes her away from him and draws his sword.

He steps forward, then his eyes widen.

Imbedded in his forehead is a star of spiked metal. He falls into Teurith, they collapse together, and she struggles underneath him. Blood from his mortal wound drips onto her.

Teurith whimpers.

"Are you hurt?" Djáraad says.

"Just get him off of me."

"Thank the Gods you're safe." Djáraad pulls Knut's dead body off of Teurith. "I have to hide him." He stoops to drag the dead body away but its flesh dissolves, steam rising from it and the skeletal remnants sink into the earth.

"Horrid," Teurith says.

Djáraad takes her arm and walks her to the small clearing. "Here. Have some of this." He breaks off some rabbit meat and helps her drink from a water flask.

"Thank you," she says, and shudders.

"We have to get moving by dawn. Eat, drink, and then sleep."

"What do we have to do to get to the river?" Teurith says.

"The falls run over a cliff and the River Rys begins at the bottom. We must climb down."

She gasps. "Climb down a cliff?"

"Yes. It's steep, not impossible. Trees growing out of it and uneven rocks make it easier to descend. There's even a path somewhere."

Teurith groans.

He rips more rabbit meat off the bone, and hands it to Teurith.

They eat in silence, then stretch out on the ground for the night.

Teurith's muscles ache from exhaustion, and sleep eludes her. She peers into the darkness, and remembers last night's dream. Who was the young woman in the mirror? She shivers as she recalls the three hooded figures, and Knut's hot breath in her ear, then turns on her side and sees Djáraad sleeping. At home in Loring, she's used to the Deafwood at night. This forest is days away from there, and she thinks of her father. Maybe they'll meet him on the road—if they make it that far.

Sunlight wakes Teurith.

Djáraad sits at the foot of a tree next to her. "I thought it best you sleep later this morning. We must continue in darkness after the sun sets."

She rubs her eyes, and drinks from her water skin. "How far is it to the cliff?"

"Not far. Then we descend. When we reach the bottom, we keep moving. By the time it's dark there won't be cover. We travel by night and stop only when we're too tired."

Teurith nods and puts her cloak on. "I'm already tired," she mutters under her breath.

The roar of water grows louder as they approach the cliff. Rock formations and scrubby trees limit their view ahead.

Djáraad slows his pace and stops. "Wait here," he says. He walks ahead and disappears behind a boulder.

Teurith waits for a moment, glances over her shoulder, then walks forward anyway. When she reaches the rock, she peeks around it and bumps into Djáraad.

"You should've waited. The ground drops off suddenly ahead."

They reach the edge and Teurith peers down. "Can't we go around?"

"It would take days of walking south. And we're on the wrong side of the river. Now we have to hang and drop to the lip below. There will be a lot of that."

Teurith gazes toward the cloudy sky beyond.

"You go first. I'll help you. It's not that far. Let me take your pouch and the sack," Djáraad says.

She hesitates.

"It'll make it easier for you if I carry them."

"Alright." She lowers herself, and grasps a root on the edge of the cliff. Then she hangs and lets herself fall, her knees flexing under her as she hits the ground.

"Good. I'll be right there." He drops beside her. "Now we climb down until we reach another lip."

"What about that path?" she says.

"I probably won't be able to find it."

They use outcroppings of rock and trees to steady themselves as they descend, zigzagging their way down. After a long while they reach a bigger lip of rock, more of a plateau. The sun is high. Teurith unfastens her cloak and it flutters around her.

"Do you need rest?"

"No. Just hot. Let's keep going," she says.

Djáraad inches along the edge of the lip and finds a suitable place to descend. "Here," he says, and kneels. "It's not as steep."

Taller trees grow from the incline as Teurith and Djáraad wend their way down, and the cliff becomes a series of tiered hills. The afternoon sun sinks lower in the sky, and shadows cross over them. They continue until they find a shallow cave.

"Let's stop here."

"For the night?" Teurith says.

"Just for a while. In the last hour of daylight, we should reach the bottom. Then we cross the plains in the dark. Hopefully, we'll make it to the forest by dawn."

They sit and eat the rest of the rabbit meat. Teurith's eyes become heavy with fatigue, and she snaps them open. Djáraad steps out of the cave, cocks his head to one side and listens. The wind kicks up and the light fades.

"Now that we're farther from the falls, it's easier to hear. All's quiet. We should go."

Teurith brushes her cloak off and follows Djáraad as he pushes the thicker brush aside so they can get through. They stumble out of a straggly bush onto a pathway.

"Here's the path, now that we're almost at the bottom," he says.

"Of course."

As the sun sets they come to the end.

Teurith glances up behind them, where the last light hits the top of the cliff. "I can't believe we just climbed down all of that."

"And the difficult part is still ahead. Stay close."

They move in darkness over the barren ground. Clouds cover the moon for most of the way and it's hard to see. Teurith trips, and Djáraad catches her before she falls.

He extends his arm. "Take my hand."

She exhales and puts her hand in his.

"Your palms are clammy. Are you cold?" he says.

"No. Just nervous."

After hours of walking east, light seeps through clouds on the horizon.

"Are we near the forest?" Teurith says.

"It must be a lot farther than I thought," he says, and glances over his shoulder. "Teurith."

"What?" She turns toward the cliffs and sees flecks of torchlight in the distance. "What do we do?"

"We have to run for it. When the sun rises they might be able to see us unless we find cover."

They run as fast as Teurith can run in her dress. Djáraad still holds her hand and keeps her steady. Ahead they see the silhouettes of giant standing stones at the top of a mound, and they run faster. They reach it and move to the other side behind one of the stones.

"We can't stay here. They'll come upon us," Teurith says.

"Catch your breath and then we go."

The rising sun blinds them as they crouch on the east side of a standing stone.

Teurith's gut swirls with fear. "There's nowhere to go," she says.

Then they hear a whoosh and a thud. The ground shakes. They huddle together and tremble as a mammoth shadow blocks the light from the sun. A huge, winged form begins to materialize.

"Gördög," Teurith whispers, wide-eyed.

"They don't exist," Djáraad says.

"Apparently, they do."

*Be not afraid. Climb on my back.*

Teurith elbows Djáraad, who stands frozen.

"It's speaking to us," he says.

She nudges him again. "We have no other choice."

*Time is short. Make haste.*

Teurith drags Djáraad with her as the beast lowers itself to the ground. With a last look to the west, they see streams of flaming arrows lighting up the darkness in the distance behind them.

*Grasp my fur. Now we fly.*

# VIII
## *Secrets*
### *The Year 532*

"You're fidgeting," Grena says.

Egrith stops twirling thread around her finger and sighs.

"Finish your sewing."

"This is pointless. Why do we have to embroider them, too?" Egrith says.

"It's not, and those in need deserve pretty things as much as anyone."

"I suppose so." She hands Grena the mitten she's stitching.

"This is good." Grena examines Egrith's needlework. "We do this to help people less fortunate than we are. The wool and leather will keep someone warm, and your embroidery might give them cheer."

Egrith tries the mitten on. "The wool does feel soft, and leather stitched to the palm of it is a good idea—easier to grasp things."

"True," Grena says. "And the green dye of the wool goes with the flowery blue trim you stitched."

"It is pretty. I'm sorry I was cross." Egrith stands and pecks Grena on the cheek. "Can I go now?"

"Yes, but stay in the castle. The clouds could burst with snow."

"Alright."

With the late autumn rains, and now snow, Egrith hasn't been to the grove and she misses Dirk. She hasn't told anyone about their trysts, not even Grena. Her name day approaches and she must attend the celebration without him. Last time they visited she gave him the crystals and he promised to keep at his reading. But it's the kisses, the sweet comfort of them, that she looks forward to.

Egrith wanders the castle hallways until she comes to the spiral staircase leading to her Grandmama's chamber in the northeast tower. When she reaches the top, she pushes the thick door, which creaks open. "Chilly," she says, and shuts the door. As she's done many times before when she visits, Egrith pulls a chair to the window, covers herself with a throw and sits. On clear days, she imagines she sees the Sounding Sea to the east.

"Today is just miserable," she says to the clouded sky. "Should've brought a scrolling crystal with me." She stands. "Perhaps Grandmama has one somewhere." She rifles through dresser drawers and a trunk at the foot of the four-poster bed, then turns toward the wardrobe.

Built-in shelves line the bottom where dresses lay, folded and preserved. Egrith opens a series of shallow drawers above the shelves, where she finds colorful silk scarves, jewelry and trinkets. "Hello," she says, and pauses to examine a small porcelain figurine, a statuesque woman with flowing black hair and a crown on her head. She puts the figure down and continues searching.

Above is another shelf at the top of the wardrobe. Egrith stands on tiptoe and reaches up, moving her hands along the knotty surface. She loses her balance and teeters, then grabs something sticking out at the upper corner to steady herself. It moves and she feels the wardrobe shift. She lets go, and steps out.

Egrith notices the wardrobe itself moved forward. She walks behind it and sees the stone walls parted. Her heart flutters with excitement and she finds a candle and tinderbox in her Grandmama's dresser, lights the candle and moves toward the dark entrance. The candlelight reveals a passageway. Cautious and slow, she ventures ahead. The passage descends in a gradual spiral. She follows it until she comes to a chamber. With the flame from the candle, she lights lanterns on either side of the opening, and enters.

The chamber, more like a cave with a high ceiling, is dank and cold. Mist expels from Egrith's mouth as she scans her surroundings. "This is odd," she says, and shivers.

A large cauldron hangs from the ceiling over a fire ring filled with vermillion-colored crystals. Along one wall stands a writing desk scattered with scrolls. She picks up a scroll. It crumbles in her hands.

The cave-chamber expands as she explores. "Strange." Queasy, she sits on a bench below a smoother, flat wall where a tapestry hangs depicting a beast she's never seen before flying over a forest toward a mountain range. When her stomach settles she examines the tapestry. The beast resembles an immense mastiff with wings, covered with fur instead of feathers. "What else can you show me, Grandmama?"

One of the lanterns goes out, and the chamber is darker again. "I should get going," Egrith says. As she moves out of the cave she turns and glances over her shoulder, listening. "Who's there?" Nothing. She moves upward into the passageway, circling in the tunnel as she ascends, and comes to Grandmama's room. She finds everything as she left it. Egrith steps around the wardrobe and then inside, where she reaches for the lever. She pulls it and feels the motion as it moves into place, the stone walls closing again.

Then she remembers. "Oh, no," she groans. As fast as she can, she runs to her rooms.

Grena stands in the doorway with her hands on her hips. "Where have you been? You and your brother are to have dinner with the King. It's time to go now."

Egrith changes her dress and brushes her hair.

"I hope you didn't leave the castle," Grena says.

"No, Grena. I—I was in the Hall of Crystals."

"I looked there. Master Arkle hadn't seen you. Egrith, dear Child, these stories of yours are too much. I should tell your father."

"No, please don't. I didn't do anything wrong. I just—wandered around."

"Go on, now. You'll be late," Grena says, giving Egrith a gentle push.

Egrith hurries to her father's rooms. Before she can knock a guard opens the door. Gareth greets her.

"Father's with his steward. Says he won't be long. Haven't seen you," he says, and they embrace. "How are you feeling?"

"I'm well, thanks. How are the barracks?"

He laughs. "Cold and damp. It's good to be with the soldiers, and…"

"And?"

He lowers his voice. "Argo is there, too."

"Don't worry, dear Brother. I'm over it. I simply don't understand why he was mean that day. We've always been friends."

"I know," he says, and hesitates.

"You know what?"

"Argo is lonely. And he must be getting desperate."

"What do you mean by that?" Egrith says.

The King enters. "We'll take dinner in my study," he says, and dismisses his steward.

Gareth and Egrith follow their father, who seats himself at a table and gestures for his children to sit as well.

"What is it Father?" Gareth says.

"Let's enjoy this hearty fare first and talk after," their father says.

A serving man approaches the table, bows, and carves the roasted chicken accompanied by turnips and carrots. He pours wine into their flagons, and places portions of meat and vegetables on each plate.

Gareth attacks his food.

"My Daughter, you must eat," the King says.

"Yes, Father." She pushes a turnip around on her plate.

"Quite different from meals at the barracks, I imagine."

Gareth looks up from his dinner and sets his fork down. "Yes, although they feed us plenty."

"My scouts inform me Incarrad City musters its forces."

"But why?" Gareth says.

"We are not certain. Lord Frolichen I of Incarrad City is a good man, a competent leader, although he is old now, and fading. It is his son, Frolichen II, who concerns me. I fear he is gullible, and hasn't much sense. We must be prepared."

"Is that why you have me training with the soldiers?" Gareth says.

"In part. It's time now. You're verging on manhood. And you will command a battalion yourself someday." The King turns to his daughter. "Egrith. How are feeling today?"

"I am well, Father."

"Aren't you excited about your ball?"

"Oh, yes. I am."

"Did you choose your dress?" the King says, with a smile.

"Grena thinks I should wear blue," she says, and sighs.

"Grena is a wise woman."

"Father?"

"Yes, my Dear?"

"What can I do if we're—attacked?"

"Don't fret about that; it's unlikely they would be so bold. If that time comes you will help organize the townspeople and get women and children safely within the castle walls."

"I wish I could train for battle, too. I can sit a horse as well as anyone, and I've read a lot of about the craft of war—"

The King laughs. "My dear Child. You're too young for such worries. Finish your supper. I must meet with the Minister of Commerce. Goodnight."

Gareth and Egrith stand. Their father rises and leaves the room. They sit again and Gareth cleans his plate.

Egrith slides her chair back and stands. "I'm not hungry. Before I leave, tell me about Argo."

"He's going to the ball."

"That's fine with me. I'll keep my distance."

"But not alone," Gareth says.

"Why should I care?"

"He asked Margrin to accompany him."

Egrith flushes. "He doesn't even like her."

"I know," he says.

"Then why?"

"Maybe because he's angry about Dirk."

"No wonder he was cross with me. All I did was prattle on about Dirk, and…"

"Egrith. You cannot continue to see him."

"Who?" she says, and plays with a lock of her hair.

"I know you and Dirk meet in the grove."

She pulls her hand from her hair and grasps Gareth's arm. "Please don't tell Father."

"I won't. But if Margrin ever found out she'd tell him immediately."

"I—I have to go now," she says, and moves toward the door.

"Take care, my Sister."

Egrith returns to her chamber and takes her cloak, throws it over her arm, and hurries through the castle to the southwest gardens. Freezing rain chills her and she dons the cloak, then steps onto the pathway that leads to an exit hidden behind bushes in the corner. She looks back once and then steps beyond the castle walls into the night.

The little light there was during the day is long gone, but she could find her way blindfolded. When she passes the inn, two men stagger out the door arm in arm, singing a bawdy song. She keeps moving until she comes to the end of Smithy Lane, hoping to find Dirk sitting outside on the bench with his pipe. He's not there, and she peers in the window. Dirk and his father sit at the table smoking their pipes; Dirk reads a scrolling crystal. After a while, his father rises and leaves the room. Egrith taps on the window.

Dirk tamps his pipe and lays it on the table. He glances up for a moment, then continues reading. She taps a bit louder. He stands, approaches the door, and opens it.

"Dirk," Egrith says in a hushed voice.

He sees her, closes the door and takes her in his arms. "You're cold." He kisses her forehead.

"It's not so bad."

"What's wrong? It's late," he says.

"I had to see you. I'll be in a pile of trouble if I'm caught."

"You should go back, Egrith."

"I came all this way."

"We have nowhere to go. We'll freeze if we go to the grove."

"How about the stable? Horse won't mind," she says.

"I reckon not."

They walk around the smithy to the stable. As they open the gate the horse stomps and whinnies. Egrith feels her way in the darkness until she reaches the stall. "Don't worry, Horse. It's just us." She scratches Horse's nose. He snorts and calms down. They settle themselves in the corner where several bales of hay provide comfort.

"Oh, Dirk. I have so much to tell you." She snuggles into his arms.

He stays quiet.

"Don't you want to hear?"

"Egrith…"

"I found a secret door in Grandmama's room. There's a chamber, a sort of cave, and that must be where she practiced her magic—what's the matter?"

"You know I love you."

"Yes, of course," she says.

"But we can't—"

"Shhh. I won't hear it." She kisses him and he responds, slowly at first, then with fervor. They lay tangled in each other's arms, and Egrith begins tugging at his clothes.

Dirk pulls away. "We mustn't."

Egrith sits up, and catches her breath. "Why?"

"Father says we have to stay away from each other."

"Yes. Your father knows. I—overheard you talking."

"He knew before it actually happened." He takes her hand. "I'm going to walk you to the castle."

"You said you love me—"

"That will never change. But we are betraying the King's trust," Dirk says, and pulls her to her feet.

They walk in silence only broken by the pattering of sleet on rooftops. They come to the southwest garden and Dirk embraces her, then Egrith disappears into the darkness beyond the castle wall.

Egrith reaches her chamber without incident and removes her cloak and boots. She wipes the caked mud off and puts them away. "Dark fog about me again," she says, and catches her reflection in the mirror. Tears roll down her cheeks as she pulls straw out of her hair. Then she climbs into bed, and sobs herself to sleep.

# IX

## *Petitioners*
### *The Year 548*

The Gördög takes off. Teurith and Djáraad cling to the fur at the top of its head. They fly high above the ground where the air is colder.

"They'll see us," Djáraad shouts.

*No. Only on the ground are we visible to others.* The Gördög yawns, high-pitched, and delicate.

"You sound like a she," he says.

The Gördög laughs. *I wondered when you would notice.*

"Then the legends are true. All the Gördög are females," Teurith says.

*Yes. Only three remain.*

"Where are you taking us?" Djáraad says.

*Somewhere safe.*

Teurith tightens her grasp on the Gördög's fur, and says, "Why are you helping us?"

*You are needed. Monumental things will come to pass. I can say no more.*

Hills roll below them and they see the river shining in the distance. The Gördög begins her descent and circles above a copse of trees below.

*The city is not far. Due east through the forest for a day. Then the King's Road. Go to King Gareth.*

"The King?" Teurith says.

The Gördög lands. They climb down from her back and step away as she materializes, heaves a mighty sigh and stretches her legs.

*My time is short. And you must go.*

"But I'm nobody. How do I see the King?" Teurith says.

*He holds court daily for the common folk who seek him.*

The Gördög's eyes droop.

"Thank you," Teurith says.

*Be brave, Teurith. I must rest. Farewell.*

Teurith and Djáraad watch her take off and she disappears into the sky.

"Now, into the forest," Djáraad says.

Behind them to the west, they see the Green Mountains on the horizon.

"How long did we fly with the Gördög?" Djáraad says.

"Hard to tell. Lost all sense of time," Teurith says.

They pass an uneventful day traveling through the woods. The next morning, they continue walking and trees become sparse. After about a mile's worth of trekking beyond the forest they move south, come to the King's Road and follow it east.

As Teurith and Djáraad near the city, occasional dwellings sprout up and peasants till the surrounding fields. They continue and a speck appears on the roadway ahead of them. It comes into focus as they walk farther east. They see a wagon pulled by several carthorses; the sound of their hooves clomping grows louder as the wagon approaches.

Teurith's heart leaps. "It might be Father," she says, and runs forward.

"Wait," Djáraad says, and follows.

She stops, and sighs as the wagon passes; a gnarled old man holds the reins.

"Not your father."

"No," she says. "Maybe he's already home in Loring."

"We have to be cautious when we encounter others."

They see the walls of the city ahead and more activity on the road. Other wagons carrying bales of hay, autumn harvest vegetables and bags of grain pass by. Individual travelers stoop under the weight of the bundles they carry. Teurith and Djáraad blend in as the road grows more crowded, and the guards at the city gates give them no trouble.

"It's mid-afternoon. We should try to see the King now," Djáraad says.

"What if he won't see us?"

"A chance we'll have to take," he says.

They walk slower as the city avenues throng with people. Tables with different wares, from soups and bread to cloth to brass trinkets, occupy both sides of each lane in front of shops. Homes of wealthy merchants and noblemen with facades painted in bright colors and trimmed with ornate, carved woodwork line the streets, along with tanneries, taverns and even a brothel; banners bearing the King's sigil, green with a white tree, hang from balconies of dwellings and establishments.

"We're close to the castle wall. Are you ready?"

Teurith adjusts her cloak and slings the pouch with the stone over her other shoulder. "Yes," she says.

Djáraad smiles and watches her stride forward, then catches up.

The castle gate is closed. They move toward the guardhouse. "Hello?" Teurith shouts.

"State your business," a guard says.

"We must see the King."

The guard laughs. "You and everyone else, little Lass."

"Please?" she says. "We've traveled so far."

The guard steps out and looks them over. "Where do you hail from?"

Teurith hesitates. "Loring," she says, keeping her voice low.

"That is a long way," the guard says, and his tone softens. "Wait here." He calls to another guard, and leaves Teurith and Djáraad with him.

After a while, the guard they spoke with returns. "The queue for petitioning the King is lengthy. You can blend in at the end of it. Leave your weapons," he says, eyeing Djáraad as he gives up his bow and quiver. "And the knife in the boot, Lad." He waits, and Djáraad hands over the knife. "Come."

Teurith pauses to glance up at the castle, its purple stone shining in the sunlight. Towers above the ramparts rise into the blue sky. She and Djáraad follow the guard, who stops before a large hall just beyond the castle entrance. The end of the line of petitioners reaches the wide doorway.

"I'll leave you two here," the guard says.

As they wait their turn, Teurith whispers, "The stone doesn't look as purple inside."

"It's not. There's a coating of amethyst crystal just on the outer walls for protection," Djáraad says.

"How do you know?"

"I've seen it before, and I heard stories. They sometimes call it Amethyst Castle."

"Father never mentioned that." Teurith notices the afternoon shadows lengthening across the stone floor. "We've been waiting a long time. Now that daylight is fading we may not get our chance."

"The King is a busy man," Djáraad says.

With only a few commoners ahead of them they're finally able to see King Gareth, a blond bearded man with kind eyes sitting on a thick, ornate wooden chair.

"Welcome," the King says, and rises to greet the next man in line. "How can I help you?"

A young man with one of his front teeth missing takes a step toward the King. He bows, pulls his trousers up higher and speaks. "Me best milkin' cow, Hilly, died t'other day. And t'other cows is weepin' fer her."

The King frowns. "I'm sorry for your loss. Rolland?"

A man in a gray robe standing next to the King clears his throat.

"Yes. Rolland. Give this man some coppers, enough for a new cow."

"Thank you, Sire," the man says, and bows several times, smiling as he walks out of the hall.

Teurith turns to Djaráad again and whispers, "He seems like a good king."

Djáraad nods, and they move forward as the final petitioner states her case.

"How can I help you?" The King says.

A young, petite woman holding a bundle to her breast steps forward. "My King," she says, and begins to cry.

"It's alright. You may speak," the King says.

"It's me baby, Sire. She—me Bubby—she's sick."

Rolland glances at the King and moves toward the woman. The King raises his hand and Rolland stops. King Gareth rises. "I am sorry for your troubles."

The woman clutches the baby closer.

"Where is your husband?"

"Died of fever not long past. No food to feed meself nor me Bubby."

"Let our healers care for the child. Rolland will see you have work here at the castle in the kitchens. I am sorry for your loss, and for you and your Bubby. You are safe here."

The woman curtsies and stops crying. Rolland leads her out of the hall.

The King sits again, rubs his forehead and looks at his final petitioners. "How can I help you?"

Teurith watches the woman and baby walk away.

Djáraad bows and starts to speak, then stops and nods at Teurith.

She collects herself and moves forward a pace. "We came a long way to see you."

King Gareth stands. "What is your name?"

Teurith curtsies, then gestures to Djáraad. "This is my friend Djáraad. He helped me find my way."

Djáraad bows.

King Gareth focuses on Teurith, and says, "And—what is your name, please?"

"I am Teurith—of Loring."

The King's eyes open wide. "Have you no family?"

"Well, we came to find my father, a blacksmith. Father is my only family."

King Gareth stands and says something to Rolland, and keeps his voice low, then the king leaves the hall.

Rolland approaches Teurith and Djáraad. "The King would have you wait for a few moments." He moves away from them, walks to the exit and moves farther into the castle.

Teurith and Djáraad stay where they are. "I don't understand what's going on," she says. "I hope we're not in trouble."

"I think we'd be in the dungeons already if we were."

After a few minutes, Rolland returns. Someone walks behind him.

"Teury!"

Teurith whirls around as her father runs towards her.

"Father," she says, and they embrace.

"Oh, my dear Girl," he says.

"You left me at the inn and Lord Magus wasn't himself and they hunted for me and three ladies were there—and that sniffing man Knut—and the blood came and I—"

Dirk holds Teurith closer and she stops speaking. "I'm so very sorry I left you there," he says. "Never again."

Teurith's entire body shakes and tears well in her eyes. Then she realizes the King stands nearby, watching. She glances at him, and bites her lip. "But I don't understand." She pulls away from her father.

King Gareth approaches them. "You are the image of your mother."

"Mother?" Teurith says.

"King Gareth…" her father begins.

"It is time, Dirk. Your daughter should know," the King says, then turns to Djáraad. "Will you excuse us? Rolland, see that this young man is comfortable."

Rolland leads Djáraad out of the hall.

"I owe you both an explanation," King Gareth says, and sits. "And our heartfelt apologies."

Before the King speaks again, Dirk says, "Are you sure?"

"Yes. My father is dead. It is time for the truth, at least in part. There's been too much sorrow. For all of us."

King Gareth stands, then paces as he speaks. "My father was a good man, a good king. The Realm prospered under his rule. But he was bound by convention."

Dirk shifts his weight from one foot to the other and waits for the King to continue.

"Teurith. It's a long, sad story. I am your uncle. My beloved sister gave birth to you." He places his hand on Dirk's arm, and lowers his voice. "This must be difficult. Your service to the Realm will not go unrewarded."

Teurith faces King Gareth. "What of my mother?"

"Now Teurith, try to be patient," Dirk says. "It is good of the King to give his time—"

"Dirk, you are my oldest friend. I am just Gareth to you." He places his hands on Teurith's shoulders and says, "My dear Child. You've been through so much. You should rest now."

"But I can't rest. I don't understand," she cries.

"You belong here. Years ago—and I am so very sorry—King Egad sent you away to live in Loring with your father."

"But why?" Teurith faces King Gareth.

The King looks at Dirk, then turns to Teurith again. "More will be made known to you at another time."

Rolland returns. King Gareth whispers something in his ear, and Rolland leaves again.

"Dirk."

Teurith's father's eyes meet King Gareth's.

"Why did you leave your daughter with this Lord Magus?"

"Lord Magus has always been a friend to us, and I trusted him. As Teury grew older I would leave her at the inn when I made deliveries to Riverton. It is true this time she was apprehensive," Dirk says, and his eyes fill.

King Gareth moves to Teurith and kneels in front of her. "What made you afraid?"

Teurith frowns. "The dreams."

"Did you tell your father about them?"

"I wanted to, but I didn't remember them well enough until I knew they were real—after I ran from the inn."

"Teurith, I am very sorry. I thought you were sick with fever dreams," Dirk says.

King Gareth rises as Rolland enters the reception hall followed by a plumpish woman. The King nods at her and she curtsies.

"I am Grena."

"I—remember." Teurith says, and stands.

"Come with me and I'll show you your chamber," Grena says and tries to take Teurith's hand.

Teurith turns to her father instead. "You should've told me. It wasn't fair you didn't."

"Try not to be angry with your father, Teurith. He has always done the best he could with you—and all else," King Gareth says.

"What about Djáraad? I would never have made it without him."

The King nods. "He can stay as long as he likes."

Grena steps forward. "He'll be comfortable with clothing, hot food and a bath."

"I'll send for both you and the young man in the morning," the King says.

With a last look at her father Teurith lets Grena lead her out of the room and into the castle. They follow many corridors, then finally up a spiral staircase and they come to a door. Grena opens it, and waits for Teurith to enter first.

Teurith glances around the room. She notices a mirror hanging over a table where a pearl-handled brush lay alongside a trinket box.

Teurith lifts the brush and runs her fingers over the pearl handle. Then she stares at her refection. *I've looked into this mirror before. Only it wasn't me.* "This was my mother's room."

"Yes. You are like her, a bit taller but you have the same features, the same beautiful hair," Grena says, and moves next to Teurith. She opens the box and lifts the top section out, revealing a compartment underneath. "Look inside."

Teurith pulls a bundle out of the box and unwraps a velvety cloth. She finds a statue of a woman with long flowing back hair much like her own. Two tiny sapphires for eyes glitter at her. "She wears a crown. Is this mother?"

"No. But your mother wanted you to have her. She's meant to be Queen Benadras."

"Queen Benadras." Teurith rubs her eyes and yawns. "I read about her in Father's scrolling crystal. He read to me before I learned to talk, and then taught me how to read. Will we remain here in the castle?"

Grena hesitates. "Your father was always kindhearted, even as a boy, and skilled in the arts of magic metalcraft, like his father before him. Whether you stay here or not is something King Gareth will have to decide."

"I don't want to be apart from him again," Teurith says.

"You've had an ordeal, and you're tired. I'll prepare a bath and you'll have supper. Then you must sleep."

Grena busies herself with the bath and Teurith examines her new nightclothes, folded neatly on the bed. She's never slept in anything but her billowy shift, which she tucks into her leggings during the day. This garment is more of a gown, pale blue, embroidered with flowers on the sleeves and around the neckline. "Pretty," she says softly.

After Teurith soaks in the bath, Grena helps her dress. On a table near the window a light supper of bread, cheese and fruit waits. Teurith sits and eats slowly, but finishes the food. "Thank you, Grena."

A green silk blanket and soft furs cover the bed. Grena pulls them back, and says, "Let me tuck you in." She pulls the coverlet around Teurith and kisses her forehead. She blows the candles out, moves toward the door, and looks back at Teurith. "So very much like your mother." She opens the door and closes it behind her.

The bed comforts Teurith, but she keeps shifting her position from one side, then to the other. In spite of her weariness, sleep won't come. Moonlight shining through the windowpane keeps her awake. She finally rises and steps out of bed. *Mother. I had a mother. And father was a commoner, mother a princess. It doesn't make sense.* She moves to the window. The City of Riverton sprawls beyond the battlements below and then the castle walls. *What happened to mother?*

With the room lit by the light of the moon, Teurith opens the trinket box where the statuette of Queen Benadras rests. She feels the weight of it wrapped in the soft cloth. She takes the bundle with her and sits on the edge of the bed. She unwraps the cloth and holds the figurine up in the moonlight. The porcelain is smooth as she runs her fingers over it.

Teurith stares at the statue, remembering from the Histories how they told of Queen Benadras, her beauty, her reign, and her skill with the arts of magic. The statue's blue eyes begin to glow, and a mist surrounds her. Through the mist, a silvery blue light fills the room and the figure of a woman materializes.

Teurith hisses her breath in.

"Princess Teurith," a voice says. "Don't be afraid."

"Are you—"

"I am Queen Benadras," she says as her form stretches to its full height, and she appears, human, and formidable.

"You're so beautiful," Teurith says.

"I do not have long. The stone. Care for the stone. It is a part of what you are meant to do on your earth walk."

"Earth walk?"

"Yes. Our souls are bonded, as is your mother's to mine, to yours, and on and on."

"You mean the stone in the pouch?"

"You'll know what to do when the time comes. Keep it with you, always," the Queen says, and her ghostly form fades.

Wait," Teurith says. "It is forged with my blood. That's what The Quenn said."

"The Quenn is wise, and yes. It is forged with our blood. I made the stone with my blood, and that runs through your veins."

Please, don't go," Teurith cries.

Queen Benadras smiles and disappears.

# X
## *Grandmama*
### *The Year 532*

"I can't stand it." Egrith paces in her chamber. "This sinking feeling, the dark fog—day after day—a constant plague." She holds her stomach. "Have to walk it off." She wanders throughout the castle, and tries to smile when she passes servants, or other ladies and lords. But her lips tremble. Eventually she reaches the stables, where Kraken lives. "Hello, my friend," she says.

Kraken keeps chewing, whinnies, then clomps toward Egrith.

"Oh, my sweet beast." She scratches the curly fur on his nose.

He snorts and stomps when she pulls her hand away.

"If only we could go back, the four of us, to when we were all just friends."

The horse nudges her.

"You'd never let me down, would you?"

She hugs the horse and walks through the stables toward the castle. Then she remembers, quickens her pace and heads for the Southwest Garden. She finds Loren sitting on a bench in the corner.

Egrith settles next to Loren in a patch of sunlight. She looks over Loren's shoulder and reads a scrolling crystal along with her. Puddles in the yard begin to evaporate as the sun dries the ground.

"What are you wearing to the ball?" Egrith says.

"Mother says I should wear my yellow dress. The trim is green and goes with my eyes."

"That'll be pretty."

"What's your dress like?" Loren says.

"I want to wear the black one, but Grena says no."

Loren shakes her head. "She's right. Your blue one is beautiful, and it shimmers in the light."

"Well, the black goes with how I feel." Egrith stands. "Listen. Since we both haven't been asked to go, we should attend the ball together."

"I didn't think of that. I'd be honored. Egrith?"

"What?"

"You haven't been looking for information on the Barkus Arts, have you?" Loren says.

"No. I found something better. I can show you. I've been going to Grandmama's chambers as I always do, but I discovered something there."

"Crystals?"

"No. Want to go see now?"

"Yes," Loren says.

"Let's leave before Margrin and her minions arrive."

They cross the garden and run into Gareth.

"Ladies," he says.

"Hello, Brother," Egrith says.

Gareth hugs her, turns to Loren and bows. "My lady," he says, and reaches for her hand. "May I?"

She nods, and blushes.

He kisses her hand and says, "Loren. I've been wondering. Will anyone accompany you to Egrith's coming-of-age ball?"

Loren glances at Egrith, who nods and shushes Loren before she can speak.

"Would you care to join me?" Gareth says.

Loren hesitates.

"It's alright with me," Egrith says.

"I would love to go with you. I'm just—surprised," Loren says.

"And why not?" Egrith says. "You're getting stronger every day, and this sunlight does you good. I'll leave you to it. I'm off to Grandmama's chambers." Egrith leaves Loren with Gareth, then walks into the castle with a smiling face for the first time in weeks. "I'll just go to the ball myself, that's all."

Sun shines through the window in Grandmama's chamber. Before Egrith opens the entrance behind the wardrobe, she peeks out the door she just came through, and listens. "Nobody's around," she whispers, then closes and bolts the door.

She opens the wardrobe and feels for the lever, pulls it, and the wardrobe shifts like it did the last time. She lights a candle and steps into the passageway. This time she notices more cobwebs, and the walls are damp. She follows the downward slope of the passage round and round. When she reaches the cave it's already aglow with a dim, blue light. The room stretches out before her, continuing to expand as she paces forward.

The cave becomes a long corridor, and Egrith sees something at the end. The more she walks, the farther away the end seems. Tapestries on the corridor walls mutate, and she stops. The mastiff with wings flies over a forest. This time, two people ride astride it. The beast flaps its wings, a storm of black clouds getting closer in the distance behind it. Egrith hears thunder boom, then lightning flashes, and the beast turns toward her; she steps back, and all is quiet again.

On another tapestry, a battle rages where men on foot and horseback clash with one another under a clear sky, the purple of the Amethyst Castle beyond. The men with armor bearing River King's sigil, green with a white tree, suffer most. Egrith doesn't recognize their opponent's sigil, yellow with a black scorpion. "Perhaps one of the southern cities?" she says.

Egrith runs, and finally sees a large chest at the end of the corridor. The blue light swirls around it, then mixes with shades of green and different hues of pink. She reaches it, stands still, and when she stretches her arm out, the chest shakes.

She steps back and shields her eyes, immersed in a rainbow of color. The trunk stops shaking, and she opens it. "Nothing but old blankets?" The chest rattles and starts to shut; the light grows dimmer, and Egrith catches the lid before it closes. She rifles through the cloth and feels along the bottom. Tucked into a corner in the back of it, she finds something.

She pulls out a green leather pouch trimmed with gold, and the light brightens again. "Not that big, but it's heavy." She closes the trunk. "Hmmm...I'll take you with me. Must be late by now." When she turns to hurry back down the corridor, she's already in the cave-chamber. The swirling light stops and the blue returns. "Strange."

Grandmama's room is dark when she reaches it. She closes the cave entrance and wardrobe then leaves, holding the leather pouch close. In her own rooms, she readies herself for bed, and hides the pouch in a drawer under her nightclothes.

Tears roll down Egrith's cheeks, and she pulls the blankets up around her chin. "Oh, Dirk." Sobs shake her body. "I don't even have you. Can't tell anyone else about the pouch." Like she does night after night for weeks, she finally sleeps, exhausted from crying.

Morning comes. Egrith wakes and stretches. She hasn't opened the pouch yet. "Tonight's the night," she says, as she wanders through hallways on the way to Loren's mother's chambers.

The castle hums with energy. Servants decorate the Grand Hall where the feast and dancing will take place the night of her coming-of-age ball. Young lords return from their training with the soldiers and walk with ladies in the gardens, some couples finding dark corners where they might steal kisses.

She climbs the stairway to the second-floor balcony above the Grand Hall, and pauses in the walkway, where she looks out from the balcony. A man on a ladder pops his head up while he strings garland along the railing. "Oh, pardon me, Princess. Good day to ye," he says, and continues working.

She smiles. "Everything is beautiful. It really is a Grand Hall now."

"Thank you, Princess Egrith," he says, and beams a smile at her.

She sees a couple sitting on a bench ahead, and stifles a groan. "Margrin. And Argo. Have to at least greet them." She approaches and stops with a curtsy.

"Well, Sister dear," Margrin says, and remains seated.

Argo rises and bows.

"It's nice to see—both of you," Egrith says.

"My Lady," Argo says, and reaches his hand out to Egrith.

Margrin gives it a little slap and says to Egrith, "You'll be on your way."

"No reason to hang around here." Egrith continues walking.

As Egrith moves down the hallway, she hears Margrin speak in a shrill voice. "You can sit now, and stop staring."

Egrith frowns. "My sister is hilarious." She sighs. "But I cannot laugh."

She reaches her destination and knocks. Loren opens the door, wearing her dress for the ball. Egrith embraces her and steps into the room, where Grena and Loren's mother wait.

"The seamstresses don't have all day," Grena says, and moves towards Egrith with a blue dress draped over her arm. "Here, put this on."

Egrith tries the dress.

"They'll have to take it in around the shoulders, and we'll have to tighten the laces on the bodice," Grena says, then her voice softens with concern. "You're pale, and even thinner."

"Don't fret, Grena. I just can't eat much these days."

"Cook will make the dumplings you like so much. I'll bring them to you for supper."

"I'm tired, and thinking of retiring after this," Egrith says, and removes her dress.

"We'll sup together first." Grena turns to Loren. "You look lovely, Child. You'll make a fine companion for Prince Gareth."

Happy for Loren and Gareth, but miserable nevertheless, Egrith makes her way to her chambers and thinks of Dirk. She recalls his strong arms holding her—and his kisses. "I shall never love again."

In the last light of day, Egrith dozes while she waits for Grena to bring supper.

"Egrith," a soft voice says.

She stands. "Who is it?"

Silence.

"Egrith." The sound of the voice is more remote, but Egrith recognizes it.

"Grandmama?"

"Egrith. Egrith," Grena says, and shakes her awake.

Egrith rubs the sleepy from her eyes. "I was just having a nap."

Grena lights a candle. "You needed it from the looks of you," she says, moves to the table and waits until Egrith sits before she seats herself. "The King feels you should not attend the ball alone."

"Nobody has asked me."

"How about that young strapper what's-his-name, the tall boy with the blond curls, and those bright aqua eyes?"

"No, thank you." Egrith smells the dumplings and it turns her stomach.

"Why not?"

"He's in love with Margrin like all the others. And he's a perfect fop."

Grena shakes her head. "Try to eat a bit, Child. I worry for you. Only two days until the festivities begin."

"I don't even want to go anymore."

"Come, come, Egrith. The ball is a celebration of you. Your father had a ball for Margrin. Now it's your turn."

"She loves this sort of thing, attention monger that she is."

"She's your sister. She loves you in her own way. Try to love her back, and keep your chin up."

Egrith sighs, and rubs her eyes.

"Is there anything you want to tell me?"

"No," Egrith says.

"Is it that blacksmith's boy?"

Egrith sniffles. "Oh, Grena. How do I—stop loving someone?"

Grena sighs and looks toward the window.

"I'll never love anyone again. It's so awful," she says as tears roll down her cheeks.

Grena takes her hand. "Many beautiful things in life are hard, but the difficulty is worth enduring. Love will come your way again when it's supposed to." She tucks Egrith under the covers. "Goodnight, sweet Child."

She sleeps—without dreams, without tears—long into the night.

Egrith wakes up surrounded by glowing colors. Darkness out the window tells her it isn't yet morning. The light is strongest by her bureau, where the leather pouch is hidden. She shudders and pulls the drawer open, takes the pouch, then reaches inside. She feels a hunk of rock, and pulls it out. The moon shines through the window.

To see better, she holds the rock up in the moonlight and it grows warm. Egrith feels roughness around the edges and a smooth center. The rock, more like a stone with a transparent center, gives off a ray of light that shines across the room.

"Egrith."

She trembles.

"Be not afraid."

A figure materializes. It's Grandmama's voice, but her body is young. She stands tall and upright, long black hair flowing about her. "Egrith, Dearest."

"Grandmama." She runs to her Grandmama and tries to embrace her, but moves through the place where she should be, and stumbles.

"I don't have long, Dear one."

Egrith regains her balance, turns around and sees Grandmama's form standing by the window.

"I am merely a shade of who I was, Egrith. When you hold the stone in the moonlight, you summon me, and others."

"You mean—ghosts?"

"Yes. I wander this castle, and am able to see what happens here, as well as some things ahead. There are others, too, who may come."

"Are the others—friendly?" Egrith says.

"Many make themselves known to comfort the living, and also give warnings."

"What kinds of warnings?"

"There will be a great betrayal. Then war."

"Is my Father in danger?"

"The Realm is in peril."

"What can I do?"

"When the time comes, you must warn King Egad," Grandmama says.

"How will I know when to tell him?"

The shade weakens.

"You're fading," Egrith says, her heart racing.

"I must go. Guard the stone," Grandmama says, and disappears.

# XI
## *Shades in the Moonlight*
### *The Year 548*

Argo nuzzles Teurith's ear and gives her nose a lick.

"I suppose you want to go out," she says, and stretches in the sunlight. "Already late. Sorry, my friend." She opens the armoire and finds leggings and a tunic. "These will do."

As they've become accustomed to doing, Argo follows her out the door and down the stairway. The castle is alive with activity as Teurith makes her way to a courtyard with trees and grassy places in their midst. She yawns and waits for Argo to sniff around until he trots behind some bushes. He returns wagging his tail and she scratches his head.

"Your clothes are very odd," a boy says.

"And what a horrible beast you have there," a girl says.

Teurith turns toward them. "How so?" she says, then faces Argo. "Sit, boy. Good dog."

They stand before her, keeping their eyes on the dog. The girl wears a long, heavy dress of burgundy velvet, the boy, knickers and a short jacket that match her dress.

"At least I won't roast to death when the sun gets high," Teurith says.

"Who are you, anyway?" the boy says.

"I'm Teurith. You?"

The girl speaks. "We don't know any Teurith."

"But we haven't been here very long," the boy says. "We're related to the King— second cousins. I'm Tomas and this is my sister, Wrenn." He starts to bow and Wrenn elbows him.

"We are from Banath Stronghold. I am *Lady* Wrenn and this is *Lord* Tomas."

"Our father was appointed to be King Gareth's war advisor," Tomas says.

"Good for you. I'm meeting my father for breakfast. C'mon, Argo."

"Hope to see you again, and I think your dog is magnificent," Tomas calls after Teurith.

Teurith leads Argo through the castle to her father's room. When she arrives, she pushes the door open and he greets her with a hug.

"Hello, my Daughter. Sit with me," he says.

"I just met the stupidest girl and boy ever."

"Now, Teury. You should make friends here."

"Not snobby, prissy sorts."

"Have breakfast, then we'll talk," Dirk says.

Teurith sits. At first, she enjoys breakfast.

Then, her father speaks. "Teurith, are you able to tell me more about your time at the inn? The King will want to know."

A chill runs up her spine. She finishes chewing, and tries to talk. But she can't.

"Teury?"

"I'm sorry, Father." She takes a deep breath. "All was well when I arrived there. Even those—women—were kind. Magus was himself at first. Then—this man, Knut, the one who traveled with the women, made me nervous. And I was right to be."

"Can you tell me more?"

Teurith's teeth chatter, and she clenches her jaw. "They were looking for me, Magus and Knut, maybe others. Somehow, I got away and the Tinkers took care of me. Djáraad came with me and he saved my life when Knut attacked me in the forest. Knut is dead."

"But these women," her father says. "What did—"

"I can't talk about them," Teurith cries.

A knocking interrupts them.

Dirk glances at his daughter, who nods, and he says, "Come in."

King Gareth enters, and Dirk and Teurith rise from their seats.

"Please, don't get up." The King shuts the door and sits.

"My new Minister of War, a cousin called Lord Tannen, is here to advise. Dirk, I want you to sit in on our conferences."

"My King, but why?"

"I want you to oversee the soldiers who will wield the new magic weapons."

"But I am not skilled in the ways of the sword," Dirk says.

King Gareth looks at Teurith. "Will you excuse us for a moment, my Dear?"

"Yes, Uncle Gareth." Teurith leaves and Argo follows her out the door.

Teurith waits and soon hears someone climbing the stairs below.

Djáraad appears. "Thought I'd find you here."

"Had breakfast with Father. He's in there with my Uncle," she says.

"I hope to speak with the King about my clan."

The door opens and King Gareth steps out. "Teurith, come in," he says, and smiles at Djáraad. "You as well, young man."

"Thank you," Djáraad says, and follows Teurith.

"Please," the King says, gesturing to the chairs. "I sent scouts to the west, and to the south. They haven't returned. Lord Tannen also sent scouts days ago, and they haven't returned either."

Dirk glances at Teurith, then at King Gareth, and says, "What do you need?"

"I'm going to assemble a small force north to ferret out this Lord Magus."

Teurith begins to shake, then breaks into a sweat.

Dirk rises to comfort his daughter, and says. "If I had been more aware, I might have noticed something was not right. And I should have protected my daughter…" He sees Teurith's pained expression. "Teury?"

Teurith rubs her eyes and turns away. "Father, how could you have known?" she says.

"Can you remember anything?" the King says to Teurith.

Teurith glances at Djáraad and hesitates. "There are things I haven't told you."

"What sort of things," Dirk says.

"Terrible things." Teurith reddens. "The three women—they came to the inn. They seemed friendly at first. Then…I thought Magus would protect me, but he didn't. So, I ran."

King Gareth furrows his brow. "Did they harm you?"

Teurith doesn't speak.

"My dear child, you don't have to tell us. Perhaps Grena can help you." King Gareth takes her hand. "They will be punished. We'll start with Lord Magus, and he will reveal who they are."

"Uncle?"

"Yes?"

She hesitates, then says, "Djáraad needs to speak with you."

Djáraad stands. "No. I don't. It's not important."

King Gareth leaves the room.

Teurith lowers her head and rests her face in her hands.

Argo paces in front of Teurith, then sits and leans against her with his chin on her knee.

"You tried to warn me before I left you," Dirk says, and hugs her. "Teurith, I am sorry."

"The dreams scared me, but I couldn't remember them, until…"

"You have the gift of prescience," Djáraad says. "Like the Quenn." He approaches them. "I vow to avenge Teurith, and kill those who made her suffer."

Teurith pulls away from her father.

Dirk stands and stares at Djáraad. "That will not be not necessary."

"It is necessary. And I expect nothing in return."

"You should wait for the King's counsel," Dirk says.

"I will do this alone."

"I am grateful you brought Teurith safely to us. But, please. Wait."

Djáraad nods. "Very well."

"I feel sick," Teurith says.

Argo licks her hand and whines.

Dirk's eyes well with tears and he embraces his daughter again. "You should rest, then, dear heart." He turns to Djáraad. "Young man? Let us find the King."

Teurith falls into bed in her clothes and sleeps with Argo curled at her feet.

*She's trapped in the room with them. They surround her. Teurith grabs the nearest thing she can find, a heavy green leather pouch trimmed with gold. She swings it round and round over her head and the women step back. The tallest of them approaches Teurith, her face twisted with rage. Teurith lets the pouch fly and it hits the woman's forehead. The woman reels from the blow, blood streaming down her face, and she falls to the floor. The other two women disappear. Teurith runs out the door with the pouch, the woman's curses following her as she flies down the stairs and out of the inn.*

Teurith wakes, blinking in the dark. The last light of the sun fades as she moves to the window. She remembers her dream, and shudders with relief. This time the dream was different, not how she thought it happened. She lights a few candles, finds the pouch and examines the leather, hoping to see traces of blood. Her face burns with disappointment. She didn't hurt the witch-woman. At least she's safe with Father in Riverton.

Someone knocks on the door. "Teurith?"

"Grena, come in."

"The King sent me."

"Yes. I'm grateful you're here. Will you sit with me for a while?"

They move two chairs near the window.

"Would you like a throw?" Teurith says before she sits.

"Dear girl, I am the one who should ask you. No, thank you."

They sit in silence until Grena speaks. "Teurith. King Gareth will love and protect you. I hope you will feel safe here. And you are always welcome to speak to me about anything."

Teurith continues to gaze out the window.

"You are strong like your mother, and also have much of her nature, her sensitivity."

"It must have been difficult for Father to do without her," Teurith says and sighs.

"Yes. I imagine it was. He always, always loved your mother."

"Grena."

"Yes, Child."

"I feel—tainted—in every way."

Grena takes her hand. "How so, Teurith?"

"Those women—they were rough with me. They tore at my clothes, and they—they prodded at me. Then the blood came."

Grena stays quiet.

"Why would they do that to me?"

"The blood. That is natural, something you will experience for many years to come. These women—how horrible. But the cruelty of their actions toward you is not your fault. You did what you could, and without your strength and common sense, it might have been worse for you. Much worse. What happened is their shame, not yours."

"There were three of them. I think they're witches."

Grena pulls her shawl tighter around her shoulders. "There is a legend of three women, from the time even before Queen Benadras' reign. The legend tells of The Three, an ancient evil. Together they are powerful, and can change form. But their magic and strength depend on certain artifacts they seek to possess."

Teurith thinks of the stone and shudders.

"Your Great-Grandmama Nora knew of this legend, I'm certain."

Argo barks, sniffs at the bottom of the chamber door and wags his tail. Teurith opens the door and Djáraad stands in front of her.

"I was just about to knock," he says.

Teurith lets Djáraad into the room and Grena rises.

"Remember what I told you, Teurith. You are not to blame," Grena says, and leaves the chamber.

"Was Grena able to help you?" he says.

Teurith sighs. "I feel some relief."

"I am glad."

They stand, awkward and quiet.

Teurith glances at Djáraad, grateful for his presence. "Let me show you something." She opens a drawer, takes the leather pouch, and removes the stone.

"A rock?"

"It's not just a rock. It—does things."

"What things?"

"Not sure." She returns the stone to its pouch. "Argo has to go out. Come with me to the courtyard."

The moon is bright and full. It illuminates the gardens; they don't need to light the torches. Teurith and Djáraad sit on a bench in the corner. No one else is around. She takes the stone from the pouch again and holds it in front of her. It reflects the moonlight, grows warm and glows.

A mist rolls into the courtyard and a young couple emerges. The pair gaze at one another and dance, moving in time to music only they can hear.

"She looks like you," Djáraad says.

Argo starts digging a hole in the opposite corner.

"Argo, no!" Teurith says, and the dog stops pawing at the dirt.

The couple stops dancing and the young man glances toward the courtyard exit. He says something to his partner.

Teurith and Djáraad hear their voices.

"Who called me?" the young man says.

"I heard it, too," the young lady says.

Teurith, wide-eyed, calls again. "Argo?"

"Who is it?" He takes the lady's hand and pulls her away from the sound of Teurith's voice. "I don't think it's safe. Someone might see us. And your father won't like it."

"I don't understand. Who are they and why are they here?" Teurith wonders aloud.

"I think they're shades," Djáraad says.

The couple fades and the mist evaporates.

"That didn't occur to me," Teurith says, and puts the stone away. "Maybe the purpose of the stone is to reveal things we can't usually see."

"That makes sense," he says. "Maybe the moonlight helps, too."

"Yes. Only at night. Let's try again tomorrow evening."

They leave the courtyard, Argo trailing behind.

"Did you and father meet with Uncle Gareth?"

"Yes. The scouts won't return for a few days. The King wants me to train with his soldiers, and also see if I have the gift needed for wielding weapons of magic."

Teurith stops walking and faces him. "Tell me of your progress with that. I wish I could train, too."

"Your time will come. There's a reason you have your gifts—and the stone."

"Father says I must make friends in the castle."

"I'm your friend," Djáraad says, his voice low.

"You're the only friend I've ever had, really," she says, and hugs him, which catches him off balance.

Teurith sees his blush over his dark skin, and she moves away, hiding her smile.

He walks her up the stairs to her chamber. "Thanks," she says. "We'll meet again tomorrow?"

"Yes," he says.

"Until then." She closes the door behind her, and sits on the edge of the bed. Argo lies at her feet. Her heart flutters as she thinks of Djáraad. "You like him, don't you—you big hairy dog?"

Argo gazes up at her, and his tail thumps on the floor.

"Yes, I like him, too." Teurith smiles.

They fall asleep and rest until morning.

# XII

## *The Dance*
### *The Year 532*

Egrith waits alone, last in the long line. Ahead of her are Gareth and Loren, and Margrin and Argo in front of them. Egrith smiles and says, "Loren, the dress is perfect."

Loren spins at the sound of Egrith's voice; her yellow dress swirls around her feet revealing green slippers that match the trim of her dress. "The seamstresses did a wonderful job. It fits like a glove."

"You do look beautiful," Gareth says, and takes Loren's hand, causing her to glance away. But she can't hide her smile.

The line finally moves forward as the music begins. Egrith hears the sustained tones of crystal-coated viols, instruments made from finely-crafted wood. The veneer of crystal stain over the wood gives the instrument a mellow resonance that echoes through the Grand Hall.

An ensemble of musicians plays different-sized viols; the biggest viols produce low tones, the smaller, higher tones. Their harmonies accompany the melodies of wooden flutes, and drums maintain a subtle rhythm as the herald announces people who attend the ball.

"Lord Poilet, of Sounding Sea Fortress," the herald's nasal voice says.

"Egrith."

She turns around and King Egad embraces her.

"I couldn't let you make your entrance alone on your name day."

"Oh, Father, thank you," she says.

The line moves and it's almost their turn.

"Princess Margrin and Lord Argo of Martoldt," the herald continues.

Argo walks just behind Margrin and she takes her time, stately in her plum-colored dress, her hair a brown pile atop her head.

"Prince Gareth and Lady Loren."

Gareth and Loren make a striking couple, he, dressed in gold and brown, she, in yellow and green. They smile at one another as they step forward.

"King Egad and the Princess Egrith."

Egrith maintains a sober demeanor as King Egad takes her arm in his.

Honored guests, lords and ladies of the castle, and the royal family take seats at a long table at the head of the Grand Hall. Delicacies of poultry, venison and beef sit on large plates, garnished with potatoes, carrots and squash. Servants bustle about and keep carafes of wine and ale filled. Tables for minor nobility and local merchants line the other walls, a large space in the middle for dancing.

The musicians play a lively selection, and couples dance. They circle their partners, then face one another, ending each musical phrase with a short clap before they approach their partners again and reverse direction.

Egrith watches from her seat, then glances down the table to her left, and notices Argo also staring at the dancers. He slouches with his arms folded on his chest, his face twisted into a grimace. To his left, Margrin chats with the man next to her, Lord Poilet.

Egrith mutters under her breath. "Why does Argo have anything to do with Margrin? He's miserable."

Margrin laughs, and her hand touches upon Lord Poilet's. He says something in her ear, and she laughs again, too loud, and strident.

"May I have a dance?"

Egrith turns to her father and her face brightens. "Of course."

They rise and King Egad escorts Egrith to the floor in time for the next dance. The musicians play slower this time. Larger viols and brass horns drone along with a soft, steady beat in groups of three. A solo from a smaller viol floats its melody above the other musical textures.

"Father?"

"Yes, Child?"

"Why is Lord Poilet here? I thought we weren't on good terms with him?"

King Egad's eyes dart in Poilet's direction. "I am attempting to remedy that situation with a treaty, and maybe more."

Egrith frowns. "What if he isn't sincere?"

"I forge this alliance for the good of the Realm. Try not to fret, my Daughter." He gazes toward the table. "Gareth's friend Argo sulks. I don't prefer him, or his arrogance."

Egrith says nothing.

King Egad and Egrith return to the table as the dance finishes. Lord Poilet stands and bows to Margrin. He takes her hand and leads her to the floor for the next dance, leaving Argo alone. Argo pours himself a generous amount of wine, drains his glass, and pours another.

The sprightly dance ends. Lord Poilet and Margrin move to the table, where Argo rises and bows to her. She rolls her eyes, and he follows her for the next dance, a slower selection. He takes her right hand in his left, and places his right hand on her waist. They move to the rhythm with grace until she says something to him. He glowers and releases her.

Egrith watches them, and although she can't hear what they're saying, she knows their exchange is heated. Margrin throws her head back and laughs, and Argo stomps to his seat. Lord Poilet joins Margrin for the next dance.

A pang of regret jabs Egrith. She excuses herself and moves toward Argo. "May I sit with you?"

He turns to the sound of her voice. "I don't know why you'd want to."

Egrith sits, and Argo waves at a serving man. "A fresh flagon, please."

"You should try and eat something. I've seen you refill twice."

"I had a late breakfast," Argo says.

The man returns with the flagon and lifts the wine carafe; Egrith stops him, and thumps her fist on the table. She makes her voice deep and says, "I'll have some ale."

The man pours the ale and Egrith takes a hearty swig that leaves foam on her upper lip.

Argo smiles.

"Ha. Almost made you laugh." She dabs her lip with a cloth.

He shakes his head. "Ale's a man's drink. But I know this, you're as brave as any of them, and you could probably drink them all under the table."

Egrith laughs, and Argo finally laughs, too.

"We should make a game of it," he says.

"What sort of game?"

"Let's refill each time Margrin sticks her snout in the air."

"Now, Argo. You've already had enough, and that isn't kind," Egrith says.

"Is Margrin kind?"

"Well—no. She isn't. But I don't think she can help herself."

They watch Lord Poilet twirl Margrin around the floor. She's taller than he is, and her pile of hair makes it more conspicuous.

"They deserve one another," she says, and laughs.

Gareth and Loren move to the floor, and hold hands. They glide to one side, then stop and clap once, spin, take hands and glide to the other side, clap and spin, then come together again. The moderate pace of the dance gives them chances to talk, although they remain silent, smiling. The tones of the crystal-coated viols pulse as the lower horns crescendo gradually.

"They look happy," Argo says.

"I'm glad. I love them both." Egrith sighs. "Argo?"

"Yes?"

"Why were you so angry with me?"

His face sours.

"Please talk to me."

He hesitates.

"What is it?" she says.

"You—you got us into trouble. We haven't all been together for months because of you."

"I'm so sorry. Really, I am. But at least you didn't fall and hit your head—like Dirk."

Argo shakes his head. "Dirk again."

"I can't even see Dirk anymore, and—"

"Well, well, my Sister. I believe you're in my chair," Margrin says, clinging to Poilet's arm. "Do you know Lord Francis Poilet?"

Egrith rises and curtsies.

"I am charmed," Poilet says.

"We were just going to dance," Egrith says, and reaches for Argo's hand. He lets her take it and she pulls him up.

"That was a good idea," Argo says.

"Saved by the dance," Egrith says.

Argo holds her close as the music begins. "I don't like the looks of him," he says.

"I don't either. Apparently Margrin does."

"He has a lot of hair but it's like someone stuck a bowl on his head and chopped off the excess."

"That is funny. He has a smug, crafty air about him I don't like," she says.

"You're right."

They continue dancing until the music stops. The musicians take a break and the herald announces dessert and entertainment. Egrith returns to her place next to King Egad.

Servants bring cups of berries and cream while mimes, jesters and men on stilts move about the dancing space. A jester juggles balls of different sizes. A serving maid dressed in a colorful frock carries a basket of flowers and places one in front each of the ladies seated at the tables.

"When they finish I'll rise and make a speech," King Egad says to Egrith. He smiles and says, "Don't go anywhere."

"Alright, father."

The juggler manages to get five balls in the air and when everyone applauds he feigns an air of surprise, then drops all of them. People laugh and clap harder.

The King rises, and people quiet down. "I propose a toast."

Everyone stands.

King Egad takes Egrith's hand and speaks. "On this momentous occasion, I ask that we raise our glasses in tribute to my beautiful daughter, Princess Egrith, on her sixteenth name day." He takes his glass and after others do the same, he lifts it in the air. "To Princess Egrith."

"To Princess Egrith!" They drain their glasses and applaud.

Egrith blushes and smiles, stretches her hands out in a gesture of gratitude, and scans the hall. Her eyes rest on Argo. He claps with everyone but maintains a serious expression.

"Let us have more dancing," the King says.

The musicians begin again and people flood the floor to participate. The jester flits among the dancers, stopping now and then to pose in odd positions as they move around him. Laughter erupts as he executes a handstand and wiggles his bare toes in the air.

Egrith laughs, too, but her face darkens when she sees Argo. He stares at her with a scowl. He was about to explain his anger when Margrin interrupted them. Argo fills his flagon, leaves the table and strides toward an exit.

Egrith fidgets with her napkin. She can't leave her own celebration so soon. The night wears on and she becomes even more impatient. When her Father finally asks Margrin to dance, Egrith waits a moment, glances around, then leaves the hall in search of Argo.

She moves through the castle for a while, then comes to a doorway that leads to one of the more secluded gardens. She peeks around the corner and sees Argo sitting on a bench with his face buried in his hands.

Egrith rushes to him. "Argo?"

"Leave me alone." He removes his hands, revealing a tear-streaked face.

"I just want to help. I like you so much, and we've always been good friends."

"You can't help me." He scuffs his foot in the dirt and faces the other way.

Egrith sits on the bench next to him, and scoots herself closer.

"Please don't do that," he says.

"Why? What's bothering you?"

He remains silent.

"Argo. Look at me."

"No."

"Where is this anger coming from?"

"Did you let him kiss you?"

"What?" she says.

"You know very well what I'm talking about. Gareth told me, because he was worried."

Egrith places her hand on Argo's back. "That's all over now. It just couldn't be," she says, and sniffles.

Argo turns to her, and his voice softens when he speaks. "I'm sorry for you. And sorry for Dirk."

"Thank you," Egrith says, and she blinks tears away.

"You're clearly not over him," Argo says.

Egrith cries.

"I—I'm sorry. What can I do?" He takes her in his arms. "There, now. I'm here for you. It's alright."

Egrith pulls back. "Do you mean that? I can't lose both of you."

"I'll always be here for you."

She tries to smile.

He caresses her cheek. "Yes. It's true. I have always…"

"You've always?"

"I have always liked you."

Egrith hesitates. "And I you."

"What I mean is—is that I love you. There, I said it."

She stares at Argo, wide-eyed.

"What's wrong?" Argo stands, and almost loses his balance. "I shouldn't have told you."

"You're just drunk," Egrith says.

"No. I'm not."

"But you're angry with me. And you were so mean," she says, and rises.

Argo gazes at the moon, which shines in a corner of the courtyard. He heaves a sigh and begins to walk away.

"Wait. Where are you going?"

He stops, his back still towards Egrith.

"Argo? Please."

He turns.

They stand and watch one another for a few moments, both breathing heavily.

Egrith starts to speak.

Argo walks to her and places a finger over her lips. He removes it and kisses her.

# XIII
## *The Teeth*
### *The Year 548*

"Rise and shine," Grena says, and opens a window. "Your father's been wondering about you."

Teurith rubs her eyes. "Good morning, Grena."

"Good morning, Child. You need a dress that suits you."

"Ugh."

"Now, now, your father wants you at the King's dinner, and we have to work fast."

"I know I need a dress; I just didn't think I'd have to wear one again so soon."

"You'll be beautiful. And your father will be so proud."

Teurith's day, upended by a bath, dress fittings, and Grena's constant hovering, flies by. She wonders about this dinner looming ahead, and who will attend. She sighs, as Grena brushes her hair.

"Ouch!"

"It's not so bad. You certainly need it."

"Did you do this to Mother, too?"

"I certainly did," Grena laughs. "You are so like her, always into adventure."

Teurith endures the brush. "Will you tell me more about her?"

Grena sighs. "Well, she was fearless. And she was beautiful. She loved to ride, and the great warhorse, Kraken, was her favorite."

"I like to ride. But we only had father's horse, Kaspar, and the carthorses."

"Your Uncle will teach you to ride like a proper lady, I imagine. There." Grena holds a mirror in front of Teurith. "Aren't you lovely."

Teurith's eyes widen, amazed by her reflection. Her long hair, let out of its usual ponytail, flows around her face and down her back.

"Now, here." Grena unfolds the dress and holds it in front of Teurith. "Your mother had a blue dress. She wore it for her coming-of-age ball."

"It is wonderful." Teurith tries the dress on. The sky blue of the fabric brings out the color of her blue eyes, her black hair a striking contrast. As she steps into her slippers, someone knocks on the door.

"Father," Teurith says, and rushes into his arms.

"Let me see you, Teury."

She steps away and twirls.

"You will be the loveliest young lady there. Come, we don't want to be late."

They arrive at the entrance of the Grand Hall, where they hear music, and guests are already dancing.

"So many people," Teurith says, and sees her uncle sitting at his place in the middle of a long table.

King Gareth nods and horns sound a fanfare. Everyone stops dancing. Once they're seated, the King rises and holds up his flagon.

A herald makes an announcement. "The Princess Teurith, niece of the King, and her father Dirk, Royal Blacksmith of Riverton."

The celebrants stand and raise their chalices and mugs.

King Gareth says, "To my dear niece, the Princess Teurith."

"To Princess Teurith," the crowd says.

Dirk walks with his daughter arm in arm and they sit next to King Gareth. She glances to the left and sees Djáraad with a rare smile for her. She smiles back and waves, stunned because he's dressed in silks of oranges and greens, his dark wavy hair and brown eyes focused on her.

"Let the feasting begin," the herald says. The horns call again and servants bear food on large trays, carrying them above their heads.

Teurith hears someone clear his throat. She turns to the sound. "Oh, hello, you're—Tomas—I remember."

Tomas bows. "My apologies. I didn't know who you were then. Your dress is lovely."

"Thank you. Your sister might even approve."

He laughs. "Will you save me a dance?"

Teurith glances at Djáraad. "Maybe."

"That would be—nice," Tomas says, and returns to his father Lord Tannen and his sister Lady Wrenn.

Teurith watches Tomas walk away and then looks at Djáraad, and he doesn't smile. Teurith stands, and points at her dress.

His face brightens.

King Gareth turns to her. "I am very happy you're here, safe and with us. You're a fine young lady. And you are so like your mother. She would be proud."

"Thank you, Uncle."

King Gareth slides his chair back, and Teurith sees his wife, Queen Loren. Her chair has wheels on it, and her eyes meet Teurith's eyes and she smiles. "Your mother was my dearest friend. I hope we can be friends as well."

"I would like that, Queen Loren." Teurith's spirits surge.

"Are you happy here?" Queen Loren says, when the musicians take their break.

"Oh, yes. It's wonderful to be with Father, and Uncle Gareth has been kind," Teurith says.

"Are you surprised by your welcome feast?"

Teurith smiles. "I am." She glances at the wheels on Queen Loren's chair, and her smile fades.

"Don't worry about that, Dear," Queen Loren says and pats the side of her chair. "I have always been accustomed to a quiet life of reading and seclusion. I was never one for adventure. Your mother was adventurous, and brave."

"What else can you tell me about her?"

"Your mother was also kind, and never excluded anyone. She befriended me just as I began to feel better and was able to get out more."

"What is your—condition?" Teurith says.

"I was a sickly child, and kept close to my mother. Then as I grew I became stronger and finally started reading in the gardens, and I met your mother. A few years ago, my legs became weak again and now I am not able to walk much at all."

"I'm sorry," Teurith says.

"I don't mind. Your Uncle is good to me, and we adjust. He had this chair made and I get around well enough. One of the healers, a strong man, helps me when I have to climb stairs."

The musicians tune their instruments and the music begins. Teurith turns, and finds Lord Tomas by her seat.

He bows. "Will you dance with me?"

Teurith looks to her father, who nods. "I—don't know how."

"It's easy. You'll get onto it." He offers her his hand.

She rises and takes his hand. They move to a corner of the dancing space and stand, watching couples glide past them.

Teurith shakes her head. "They all look so natural. I don't think I can do that."

"Yes, you can. Here," Tomas says, and places one hand on her waist and takes her other hand in his. He leads her, and although she stumbles at first, she gradually follows him as he steps back, then forward, in time to the music.

"What's your dog's name?"

"Argo," she says, trying to focus on the dance.

"After Lord Argo, who died in the Battle of Sounding Sea Fortress?"

"I suppose so, although I don't know the story. My scrolling crystals only hold histories from before Lord Argo's time. He was my Father's good friend."

"Your father, the blacksmith?"

Teurith stops. "Yes. My father the blacksmith. And I know. He's a commoner. But he's also Uncle Gareth's friend." She moves away from Tomas towards the table.

"I didn't mean anything by that," he calls after her.

Teurith returns to her place at the table and notices Lady Wrenn frowning at her as Tomas takes his seat.

Dirk leans closer to Teurith and says, "Teury, what's wrong? You looked as though you were enjoying yourself."

"It was alright. I'm simply not good at it."

"Dancing is a skill you must have. You're a lady of the court now, and you should make friends with the others. And this Djáraad…"

Teurith glares at her father. "What about him?"

"Again, I am grateful he brought you here and kept you safe. But you're growing into womanhood and must think of the future."

"What does that mean? You're a commoner, and you and mother—"

"We won't speak of this now. There's more to the story."

"What story? You've always kept things from me. I hope from now on you'll tell me the truth."

"Teury…"

She rises from the table and runs, her dress trailing behind her.

Djáraad rises and follows Teurith out of the Grand Hall.

"Teurith, wait," Djáraad says.

She stops and spins around to face him.

"What happened?" he says.

"It's Father. He doesn't—approve of you."

"I understand. I'm not of your kind."

"But it doesn't matter," she says, and tears fill her eyes. "You—protected me, and your people are wonderful. Jesmane, and The Quenn…"

"Yes. My clan. We take care of our own, and they accepted you because you were in need—and because you're extraordinary."

Teurith wipes tears from her eyes. "Thank you. Let's go get the stone from my chambers. That's the only thing I want to do now. And only with you. I mustn't tell anyone else."

They hurry upstairs. Teurith opens her chamber door and finds the green leather pouch. She returns to Djáraad and they head for the secluded courtyard. They move into the gardens, and through the evening mist.

"There isn't much light," Djáraad says.

Their eyes adjust to the darkness and they find the stone bench in the corner where they sat the other night. After a while the clouds part, revealing the moon. It soon disappears.

"I don't think we'll have any luck. Let's try anyway," Teurith says. She opens the pouch and removes the stone. This time as the stone grows warm in her hands it expands, then shines its own light, projected on the wall in front of them.

The light on the wall shimmers and a scene appears. A host of tiny figures emerges, and begins to move, then grow bigger.

"It looks like a battle," Djáraad says, and approaches the wall.

"I can't see it clearly. Tell me what's going on."

"There are—two armies. I don't recognize one of the sigils but the other is King Egad's."

"Green with a white tree?"

"Yes. And his army is getting beaten down. There are bodies of dead horses and men."

"What's the sigil of the opposing army?" Teurith says.

Djáraad studies the scene. "Their armor is black. Wait. I see a yellow banner. Looks like something is stitched on it, black against the yellow."

The images come into focus, and become larger. A giant black warhorse charges through the melee, then turns toward Teurith and Djáraad. The rider barrels at them as they watch. He holds an ax in one hand and a sword in the other. He approaches, hacking at Riverton's soldiers along the way as he gets closer. His helmet has a spike on the top. They see his face, pale except for the black tattoo on his forehead, the downturned corners of his mouth a twist of malice.

"I think he sees us," Teurith says, and trembles, the stone hot in her hands.

"How can he?" Djáraad leaps back from the wall.

"Look."

The sound of the horse's hooves pounding on the ground fills the courtyard, overpowering the screams from the wounded. The tattooed man leers, a black scorpion on his forehead now visible.

"Gods!" Teurith says.

The horseman's mouth drips with blood.

"Look at his teeth," Djáraad shouts, and runs to Teurith.

"Fangs," she says, and cowers, but she can't tear her eyes away.

"Drop the stone!"

Teurith lets the stone fall and darkness fills the courtyard again. All is quiet.

They hold one another as the clouds part and reveal the moon.

Djáraad pulls away from Teurith. "Are you alright?"

She nods. "Horrible. He could see us."

"Put it away. We shouldn't try that again until we learn more about it."

Teurith picks up the stone and feels its rough edges, then the smooth center. "It's not warm anymore." She opens the pouch and places it inside.

"Teurith, there you are," Dirk says, walks into the garden, and takes her hand with a scowl at Djáraad. "The King wants to see us in his chambers. All of us."

"Why?" she says.

"I don't know. You should never have left a celebration in your own honor. The King was not pleased. Manners are important. That was rude, Teury," Dirk says.

Teurith tries to keep pace with her father's long strides.

Djáraad catches up and walks alongside them. "That was my fault, Sir. It won't happen again. Perhaps I shouldn't come—"

"King Gareth asked for you as well," Dirk says with tension in his voice.

They reach the King's chambers and the door is ajar. Dirk hesitates. A guard steps out the door and ushers them inside, then into the King's study, where Lord Tannen sits with King Gareth at a large table studying a map.

Dirk stands waiting with Teurith and Djáraad.

"And we'll bring your battalions here. If the exchange goes awry, we'll crush them between us," Gareth says, notices Dirk and the others, and then rises from his seat. "This is Lord Tannen, my new Advisor of War."

Dirk and Djáraad bow and Teurith curtsies.

"Thank you for coming so quickly. We need to plan ahead. Forces are mustering in the south."

Dirk shifts his gaze from King Gareth to Teurith.

"You should all be here," King Gareth says with a glance at Djáraad, then his eyes rest on Teurith. "My niece. You have been brave; I commend you for it. And although I do not want to upset you, the time has come." He puts his hands on her shoulders. "Will you please tell us anything you know of this Lord Magus?"

Teurith breathes harder for a moment as her heart races. She looks at Djáraad and they lock eyes, then her pulse slows. "My King—Uncle—yes. I will tell you what I know." She moves forward and Gareth offers her a chair. "No, please. I'll stand."

"As you wish. When you're ready."

Teurith tells her story, from the time her father left her at the inn, through her time with Djáfaad as her protector, the Gördög, and finally reaching King Gareth's castle. She makes no mention of the stone and its strange powers.

"Why do you think these women came to the inn?" the King says.

"I don't know. They were nice at first, then they—they changed. It's like they were witches."

"And Lord Magus?"

"He was kind as always—until the end. Then when I ran from the inn and saw him he was—evil. I heard his voice calling my name after I ran away. But then I didn't trust him and kept going."

"We will find them," King Gareth says, and hugs Teurith. "Djáraad, I have news." The King hesitates.

"Of my clan?" Djáraad says.

"One of our scouts returned, and he is mortally wounded. I spoke with him before he faded. Young man, I'm afraid your clan suffered losses, and few of your people remain. The other scout is leading the rest of them here."

"Who did this?" Djáraad says.

"Marauders from the south travel in small bands, and set out to wreak havoc upon those they encounter. We believe a Duke Fengan united groups of these cruel raiders to do his bidding."

"I have to do something. I…" He shields his eyes with his hand.

"I am truly sorry for your loss. We seek to avenge you—and Teurith. I hope you will remain here with us, and train our soldiers in the arts of your weapons. You have great skill."

Teurith moves to Djáraad, and places her hand on his arm. "I am very sorry, my friend. But please. Listen to my Uncle."

He turns toward King Gareth. "I will wait, and do as you ask." He takes a deep breath and exhales. "What of this Duke Fengan?"

Lord Tannen stands and looks at the King, who nods. "After the battle of Sounding Sea Fortress in the Year 533, this man led the remnants of the enemy army to the south, on the southern side of Crispan Bay. We knew nothing of him until recently, other than he was a demon of a warrior in battle."

Teurith approaches King Gareth. "Uncle?" She glances at Dirk. "And Father?" They wait for her to speak. "May I be—excused?"

"If your Uncle Gareth says it's alright."

King Gareth nods.

"Thank you," she says, and walks toward the door.

Djáraad follows her.

"Young man," Dirk says.

Teurith is already out the door and Djáraad ducks his head back in after Dirk calls, long enough to hear King Gareth's reply.

"Dirk. Let them be. They're friends, and need each other. You must remember that much, when we were all so young…"

Djáraad reaches Teurith and she buries her face in his shoulder. "I'm sorry for your loss."

"I shall avenge them." He pauses. "We will." He holds her closer. "You're brave; always remember that. And my clan would be fortunate to have someone as strong as you. If they—could survive this somehow."

Teurith places her hand on his cheek. "I'm so very sorry about your family."

"I know."

"Do you want me to come with you when you go to them?"

"No, thank you. You need rest." He embraces her. "I respect King Gareth. I will serve such a man. And…"

"Yes?" Teurith says.

"And, I do this for you." He kisses her forehead. "I will always be by your side."

Teurith tries to smile.

"I'll walk you back to your rooms before I see my family."

"No. You must go." She watches Djáraad move down the hallway and around the corner.

Teurith reaches her chamber, opens the door, and Argo bounds over to greet her.

"Thank the Gods for you."

He wags his tail, jumps on the bed and curls up at the foot of it. Teurith changes into her nightclothes, rubs the dog's soft fur behind his head and climbs in herself.

# XIV
## *Betrothals*
### *The Year 532*

Egrith returns Argo's kiss.

He traces the smooth skin from her chin down her neck, and runs his fingers through her hair.

Then she pulls away.

"What's wrong?" he says, breathless.

"It's—too soon."

"Why?"

"I feel like a part of me died when—"

"When what? Is this about Dirk?"

Egrith hesitates. "I'm sorry. I was comfortable with him. And I didn't expect you to like me, and I'm confused, and I want you to kiss me, but I feel bad about it."

Argo sighs and takes her hand. "We can just sit if you want."

In the quiet of night, they hold hands. The moon breaks through the clouds, shining on their faces. After a while they hear voices, and retreat to a corner of the yard behind a cluster of bushes.

"What's Sounding Sea Fortress like?" Margrin says.

"I hope you'll come and see for yourself," Lord Poilet says.

"I would love that."

Margrin and Lord Poilet sit on the bench where Egrith and Argo just sat.

He pulls a small bundle out of the pouch attached to his belt. "I have a gift for you."

"Oooh, what is it?"

"Close your eyes."

Margrin obeys.

Lord Poilet unwraps a piece of cloth. He leans toward Margrin and circles her neck with a pendant, and fastens the chain behind her. "There."

The heavy jewel hangs between her breasts. She examines it. "How opulent, and lavish."

"It was my mother's. It matches your eyes and the waters of the sea."

"I love it," she says.

"I will speak with King Egad formally. First, I ask that you come with me when I leave, and be my betrothed."

Margrin tries to kiss him.

He pushes her away. "Not yet. We must wait. I'll speak with your father."

"Soon, please."

They rise and leave the courtyard.

After the sounds of voices recede, Egrith and Argo step from behind the bushes, and return to the bench.

"What does she see in him?" Egrith says.

"And what does he see in her?" Argo says, and laughs.

"Father may have planned this. You know, when Lord Poilet saw Margrin with you, it may have roused his appetite."

"Ah. So, I was the dupe."

"Look at it this way. At least you don't have to kiss Margrin," she says.

"You're right." He pulls Egrith close.

"Argo?"

"Yes?"

"Let's try again." She kisses him.

They stay long into the night, and only stop when the moon disappears behind the taller trees in the courtyard.

"When do you return to the barracks?" Egrith says.

"Not until after the equinox celebration. Then we resume our training."

"Good. We have almost two months. I have an idea."

"What?"

"I found something in Grandmama's chambers and haven't told anyone, not even Loren. I can show you," she says.

"Alright. When, and where is it?"

"Her rooms are in the Northeast Tower—the giant round one. How about tomorrow afternoon?"

"Yes. I'll walk you to your rooms."

"No, Argo, please. Father wouldn't approve, and Grena might be waiting for me. It's late."

He kisses her. "Very well. I will see you tomorrow."

"You leave first. I'll follow after."

Egrith waits for a few minutes, then rises and moves into the castle. She follows different passageways until she comes to the entrance to the Grand Hall, where servants clear the tables in the wake of the celebration. By the time she climbs the stairwell to her chamber, her eyes begin to droop. She opens the door and sees Grena dozing in a chair, peaceful in the glow from a candle. Egrith tiptoes around the room and changes into her nightshift, then leans over a basin and washes her face.

"It's near dawn," Grena says.

She turns and pats her face with a cloth. "I was trying not to wake you."

"Your father was concerned and sent for me to wait here until you arrived."

"Don't worry. I didn't leave the castle."

"Where were you?"

"I was in the courtyard gardens. Northwest wall."

Grena sighs. "Child, you were not seen there. Your sister Margrin looked for you, too."

"Well, I was there, because we saw Margrin with that disgusting Lord Poilet."

"And who's we?"

Egrith hesitates.

"Well?"

"I was with—Argo."

Grena shakes her head. "You know the King does not approve of him."

"He's Gareth's friend."

"That's different. They're young men. You're not children anymore. It's unseemly to continue as you were, making mischief, gallivanting about the countryside."

"I'm sorry. I'll speak with Father, and try to reassure him."

"You're a good girl, and you know what's right."

Egrith looks away, toward the window. "Yes."

"Now, try and sleep." Grena guides her to the bed, and tucks her under the covers. "Rest well, Child."

"Thank you, Grena. Goodnight."

Grena leaves.

Egrith stares out the window at the burgeoning dawn, the sky streaked with pinks and purples. Her body relaxes under the weight of fatigue, but her mind remains active with thoughts of Argo's kisses and his arms around her. Then dread emerges as she thinks of facing her father. She finally drifts into sleep as the sun rises.

The sound of water pouring startles her awake as a servant changes the water in the basin, and then replaces the chamber pot. Egrith sleeps again.

"Time to get up," Grena says, and pats Egrith's arm where it hangs over the edge of the bed.

Egrith sees Grena and sighs. "Sleeping." She rolls over on her other side.

"It's after noon. You're to sup with the King. Come, now."

The dread feeling returns.

"What's wrong, Dear?" Grena says.

"Is he angry with me?"

"I believe he simply wants to discuss some things, not scold. I'll help you dress. There isn't much time." Grena takes a rose-colored dress from the wardrobe while Egrith washes. "Hurry, he's waiting." She helps Egrith pull the dress over her head and fastens the laces, then brushes the tangles out of her hair.

"Ow," Egrith says.

"If you'd brush it before you sleep you wouldn't have so many knots." Grena continues until Egrith's hair is smooth and shiny, flowing down her back.

"Will you come with me?"

"No. I have things to do. You'll be fine," Grena says, hugs her, and they part at the bottom of the stairwell.

When Egrith reaches her father's chambers the door is open, but she knocks before she enters.

King Egad rises from his chair. "Daughter." He embraces her. "Come with me, and let's sit by the window. The day is beautiful."

Egrith follows him to a chair alongside his.

"Please, sit." The King waits for her to sit before he speaks. "Egrith, I am proud of you and the young lady you're becoming. It is important, however, that you act the part. You have responsibilities to the Realm. Your sister understands this. I must impress upon you the importance of it as well."

"I understand," she says.

"When the time comes you must marry, and strengthen our bloodline for the good of all."

"Like Margrin and Lord Poilet?"

"How do you know of this?"

"I—was in the courtyard and heard them talking," she says.

"And were you alone?" King Egad says, his tone of voice stern.

"No."

"Who was with you?"

Egrith lowers her head. "Argo."

"As I've said before, you're not a child. Argo is skilled with the sword, and he's Gareth's loyal friend. He can remain here in Riverton and continue his training. But he has an arrogance about him I do not appreciate. He oversteps his bounds."

Egrith stays quiet.

"Margrin will soon leave for Sounding Sea Fortress with Lord Poilet and maintain her chastity there until after the wedding feast. Someday I'll find a suitable man for you as well, someone who will cement an alliance with Riverton for the common good."

"But what if something goes wrong?"

"What could happen?"

Egrith thinks of her Grandmama's warning of betrayal. "What if Lord Poilet is— untrustworthy; what if he doesn't mean well?"

"I have nothing to fear from him. Lord Poilet needs this alliance with us, even more than we do."

"Yes, Father."

"Chin up, Egrith," he says.

She makes eye contact, her eyes full.

"There, there. Try not to cry." He rises from his seat and takes her hand.

Egrith stands. "I'm sorry, Father."

The King takes a cloth from his pocket and dries her eyes, then hugs her again. "Now go my brave girl, and enjoy what's left of the day."

She leaves the King's chambers. Once the door is shut behind her she pauses, and leans her back against a wall. She holds her hand to her forehead and shakes her head. "I am not my sister." With steely resolve, she makes her way to Grandmama's chambers, where she finds Argo waiting.

"I didn't think you'd make it," he says.

"We have to be careful, and only meet here. Father will know if we meet elsewhere. This tower is out of the way and people rarely come near."

They move into Grandmama's room.

"Looks ordinary enough in here," Argo says.

"You'll see." Egrith gestures as she paces around the room, and points to the walls. "Notice how the room seems smaller than the size of this tower? Now, watch." She climbs in the wardrobe and reaches for the lever. The wardrobe shifts and reveals the hidden passageway.

Argo whistles. "Amazing."

Egrith lights a candle and they move through the entrance, parting cobwebs as they walk down the tunnel toward the first chamber. The stone walls of the passage become less rough, and slick with damp. They watch their footing as the tunnel slopes and turns, and they come to the cave-chamber.

Argo approaches the cauldron hanging from the ceiling. An orangey light radiates from the crystals underneath. Egrith turns toward the cauldron and drops the candle, which extinguishes as it hits the floor.

"Strange," she says. "Those crystals didn't glow when I was here before."

Argo reaches for her in the dim light. Egrith shivers as he wraps his arms around her. He buries his face in her hair and inhales the scent. They stand in an embrace until she pulls away. He looks toward the pile of cushions in the corner of the chamber; Egrith follows his gaze.

"We shouldn't," she says.

"I know."

Music, soft and lilting, fills the room.

"Where's that coming from?" she says.

"I can't imagine. But I adore you. I always have. For now, just dance with me." Argo puts a hand on her waist and takes her other in his free hand. They move in time to the music's slow tempo, back and forth.

As they gaze into one another's eyes he caresses her back and she leans into him. Their bodies are as close as they can be, and he kisses her once again. Their kisses become more impassioned, and the light from the crystal embers begins to fade. The music grows softer.

Argo pauses, and whispers in her ear. "To you, my Egrith, I pledge my troth."

"To you, Argo, I pledge my troth." She kisses him again.

They continue the dance until all is quiet.

"We should go before the crystals fade completely," Egrith says, and lights the candle she dropped earlier.

"Yes, I suppose so." Argo embraces her after they return to the room with the wardrobe.

They part and agree to meet again. A few days a week they find one another at Grandmama's chambers, always dancing, talking and growing closer.

Between meetings, Egrith sleeps, takes meals with her Father and Gareth, and sometimes, Grena. She reads in her rooms and maintains a façade of good behavior.

One afternoon as they dance, the music fades earlier, and Argo pulls her towards the cushions in the corner of the cave-chamber. Egrith does not resist.

After a long while Egrith sits up, sighs, and lowers herself again, nestling in his arms.

"I wish we could stay like this forever," he says.

"And I as well." She blushes and smiles. "I had no idea."

"What?"

"That was—otherworldly."

Argo reddens, and kisses her again. "I'm sleepy."

"Yes, and it must be late." Egrith rises from the pillow and pulls Argo up with her. They dress and she kisses him once more. With just enough glow to see by, she lights a candle, takes his hand and they leave the cave-chamber.

"Tomorrow," he says, as they approach the wardrobe.

"Yes."

Argo leaves her watching after him, and she pulls the lever that closes the hidden entrance. After a few minutes she returns to her own chamber and changes for bed, thoughts of Argo's lean body molding perfectly with hers as she drifts off to sleep.

# XV
## *Competitions*
### *The Year 548*

Teurith waits with Wrenn while Tomas mounts. Djáraad already sits his horse, like he belongs atop the thick, leather saddle.

"How will you ride with that dress?" Teurith says.

"It divides so I won't have to sit to one side," Wrenn says, and shows Teurith her skirts, more like billowy trousers.

Teurith watches as Riding Master Lan places a saddle on one of the smaller horses. He shortens the stirrups, and helps Wrenn up.

"Your turn," Master Lan says, and leads Teurith's horse to her, larger than Wrenn's.

She hesitates.

"Don't be afraid. She's a gentle giant," he says.

"It's not that. Father's horse Kaspar is even bigger than she is."

"Then, what?"

"It's the saddle. I've never tried one."

"You'll get on to it. And did you say Kaspar?"

"Yes," she says.

"Hmm."

He helps Teurith mount and she frowns.

Master Lan mounts his horse and leads the party out of the stables. Tomas rides ahead with Wrenn and Djáraad follows. Teurith keeps apace with Master Lan. Hills roll under them as they ride east. A stone wall stretches out ahead of them. Tomas spurs his horse forward and jumps the wall with ease, and Wrenn, not far behind, flies over it as well. Djáraad circles back to Teurith and Master Lan.

"Keep going, light on the reigns. The horse will know what to do," Master Lan shouts.

Djáraad quickens his pace, posting in his saddle, and jumps the horse over the wall.

Teurith's palms sweat as she runs the horse faster. She approaches the wall, hesitates, and the horse stops short, almost throwing her.

"Are you alright?" Master Lan says.

"I've never had to use a saddle before. Kaspar always knew what I wanted."

"I'll see what I can do for next time," Master Lan says. "Would you rather not ride today?"

"No. I just miss my Kaspar."

That afternoon, Teurith and Djáraad meet in the expansive training yard in front of the barracks. A series of targets stand in front of the wall that surrounds the yard. Young men practice with bows and arrows and others train with swords. Lord Krimpt, the leader of First Battalion, strides toward them, the jewels on the hilt of his sword gleaming in the sunlight.

"Djáraad, you continue with the fledglings of Third Battalion. Lord Tomas, you take the swordsmen of Fourth," Lord Krimpt says, his voice booming over the yard. He turns to a group of younger men milling about by the barracks. "Ho! Tenderfeet. Move." The young men come to order and line up, some with Tomas, and others in front of Djáraad.

Teurith moves to take her place among the men of Third Battalion.

Lord Krimpt stops her and says, "Not you, Lass. I'll have a word." He walks to a far corner of the yard out of earshot.

Teurith follows, then stands before him.

"I've been watching you these last three weeks. I did not think you would be able to keep up with the soldiers." He pauses.

Teurith waits.

"I see you work, harder than the others even, and you're quick on your feet, smart and accurate."

"Is there a problem?" she says.

"You must show them your skill. You'll train the men with the new weapons. Your father is bringing them today. He'll be here any minute."

Teurith sees Dirk walk through the gate carrying two bulky sacks in his arms. She runs to him.

Dirk glances at Lord Krimpt, who nods.

"Teury, I made something for you," Dirk says, and opens the first bundle. He holds a chainmail shirt up in front of her.

"It's beautiful," she says, and feels the smooth purple links, set with gems of different hues.

"It's coated with amethyst and woven with spells for protection. Try it."

Dirk helps her slip the shirt over her head.

"Doesn't feel like I'm wearing anything at all."

Lord Krimpt nods his approval. "The lads will start training in their armor soon. You wear this from now on."

She nods.

Lord Krimpt continues speaking to Dirk. "Did you finish the star-discs?"

"Yes, Lord."

"Teurith will train the men today."

Teurith takes the sack from her father.

"I made the star-discs using the sharp, star-weapons Djáraad brought with him as a paradigm. Remember," Dirk says. "They're only small discs of crystal until you release them with intent. Then they become weapons, larger pointed stars, as they fly through the air and head for their targets."

"Yes, Father."

She walks toward Third Battalion with haste. Djáraad shouts instructions at the soldiers. They practice clashing swords in pairs or small groups. Teurith approaches, and as the men notice her, they stop their fighting and stare. Djáraad sees her and stops shouting.

Teurith takes a deep breath. "Carry on." She observes the soldiers' training exercises as they continue practicing.

Djáraad stands beside Teurith. "Your presence makes a strong impression and—you're shimmering. Show them your skill with the star-discs."

"Very well," she says.

"Let them get used to you."

"Come to order," Teurith shouts, and the soldiers stop sparring and line up. She moves in front of them and opens the sack of star-discs. She scans their faces as she speaks. "Look at the targets." She pauses. "Before you let the star-discs fly, imagine them hitting the heart of your enemy."

"What's that supposed to mean?" one soldier asks. Others snicker.

"You have to make it happen, will it to happen, or you'll miss," Teurith says.

"That sounds like flowery woman-talk," another young man says.

Some soldiers laugh.

"I'll show you." Teurith turns towards the targets. She takes a star-disc from the sack, then flings it with a snap of her wrist to the far target on the right. In mid-air it becomes a sharp, larger pointed star and embeds itself in the center of the target.

"That's just luck," a young man shouts from the back row of soldiers.

Soldiers from Fourth Battalion, including Tomas, stop clashing swords and pause to watch Teurith working with Third Battalion.

Teurith reaches in the sack for another disc, pivots quick and sure, and lets it fly. It hits the wooden beam just above the man who taunted her, and he looks behind him, wild-eyed.

Djáraad turns to address the young men. "I, for one, would take her seriously."

Tomas shouts across the yard. "I would, too."

"Teurith, continue," Djáraad says.

The soldiers murmur.

She returns to her place in front of Third Battalion. "As I said, you must see your target, imagine yourself hitting it, and do it. Doubt will be your downfall."

Djáraad and Teurith move from man to man, handing out the crystal star-discs.

"Remember these are merely smooth discs until you let them fly. If you focus on your target, the discs alter and become the larger spiked stars—like the one you see stuck in the beam above that soldier's head."

Some of the men chuckle.

"You will each be given a pouch of ten stars. You must learn to make every one count."

They practice throwing the discs, some hitting the targets, and some of the discs thrown lose their momentum before they reach the goals. At the end of the training session Teurith collects the discs and puts them in the sack.

"That's all for today," Djáraad says with his eye on Teurith.

She moves through the throng of soldiers and the crowd parts for her. Then they disperse and leave the yard for the barracks.

Teurith lingers in the yard, waiting for Djáraad and Tomas.

Djáraad finishes realigning the targets and approaches her.

Tomas joins them, and says, "You were wonderful today."

"They were skeptical."

Djáraad considers. "Perhaps at first, but didn't you see how they made way for you? Teurith. You have a glow about you. With that and your skill they will listen to you, follow you."

"The chainmail shirt helps," Tomas says. "You know, making you look more like a soldier. But Djáraad is right. You do glow, even without the chainmail."

Teurith sighs. "I have to go. Meet in the dining hall?"

"Yes, see you there," Tomas says, and he and Djáraad watch her leave.

Teurith washes, changes into a simple, green dress and heads for supper. In one of the passageways she runs into Wrenn, also on her way to the dining hall. Wrenn's dress is more ornate, gray with blue trim, and it trails behind her.

"You look pretty," Wrenn says. "Green's a good color for you. Makes your eyes bright."

"Thanks. You, too."

"Tomas says you stunned everyone today during training, almost killed one of the soldiers who made fun."

"Tomas exaggerates," Teurith says.

"Let me tell you something. You are skilled with weapons. But don't try to hide your beauty. You can use it as an advantage."

"What does that mean?"

"Keep doing what you're doing. Now that they're impressed with your skill, allow yourself to smile at them, bat your eyelashes, speak sweetly."

"Yuck," Teurith says, and stops walking.

Wrenn faces her. "Then you'll have their loyalty, too."

They reach the dining hall, see Tomas sitting with Djáraad in the corner and join them. Teurith focuses on the meal before her, and Wrenn talks with Djáraad as she sups. Tomas stays quiet. A pang of regret stabs Teurith as she listens to their chatter.

"And were you afraid?"

Djáraad considers. "Yes. But you can't let fear stop you. As Teurith said today, doubt will be your downfall. Isn't that right?" he says to Teurith.

"Yes," she says.

"It's true for everything, not only fighting," Wrenn says, twirling a lock of hair around her finger, as Djáraad gazes at her. "You have to imagine yourself having what you want, and it'll come to you." She smiles at Djáraad.

He glances at Teurith, who rolls her eyes.

Tomas finally speaks as he rises from the table. "I'm tired. See you in the stables first thing tomorrow."

The others wave their goodbyes.

Teurith finishes her supper and continues listening to Wrenn and Djáraad, who says something and she giggles.

"Time for me to go," Teurith says.

Wrenn whispers in Djáraad's ear, then stands.

Djáraad turns red, and tries to hide a smile.

Anger swells within Teurith, and she quickens her pace.

"Wait for me," Wrenn shouts across the hall, and runs to catch up with Teurith.

Teurith ignores her.

"Hey, there," Wrenn says.

Teurith stops walking, and spins to face Wrenn. "What?"

"There's no need to be rude."

"What are you doing?"

"Whatever do you mean?" Wrenn says.

"Will your father actually allow Djáraad to court you?"

"Of course not."

"Then why do you push yourself on him?" Teurith says.

"Don't be a child. There's nothing wrong with a little fun."

"At Djáraad's expense."

Wrenn flips her hair over her shoulder. "I'm sure he can take care of himself."

"Yes, with his skill for weapons and leading the soldiers. But he lost much of his tribe. His heart may be fragile."

"Listen to me. Do you think your father, although a commoner, will let you consort with Djáraad? Your father sets his sights higher. You'll see I'm right," Wrenn says, and leaves Teurith standing alone.

The following morning Teurith takes her time getting to the stables. Tomas, Wrenn and Djáraad are already there waiting. Tomas stands off to the side, and Wrenn, svelte in riding leggings like Teurith's, talks with Djáraad, who can't take his eyes off her.

"Oh, brother," Teurith mutters.

Riding Master Lan readies horses for all except Teurith. The others mount and leave the stables for the fields beyond the castle walls.

Master Lan disappears around a corner as Teurith waits. He soon returns leading a large, tan-colored horse.

Teurith's spirits lift. "Kaspar!" The horse whinnies and stomps his foot, then moves next to a gate. Teurith steps up the rungs, and Kaspar stands still when she's high enough to climb on his bare back. "Let's go," Teurith says, clutching Kaspar's mane. The horse trots out of the stable and begins to canter, eventually breaking into a gallop. Teurith's heart soars and she laughs as Kaspar flies faster.

Ahead of her Tomas gallops, with Wrenn and Djáraad riding in front of him. Teurith catches up to Tomas. They slow their pace and shout greetings at one another.

"Your sister is overstepping her bounds," Teurith says above the beating of hooves.

"You mean Djáraad?" Tomas says.

"Yes."

"She always gets what she wants."

"Are you angry with him?"

"No. Why would I be?"

"You seem upset, and I thought maybe it's because he and your sister have been rather friendly."

Tomas' expression sours. "That's not his fault. She's a colossal flirt."

"I gather that. She isn't even serious about him—just wants to play."

"I don't think he cares for her. It's not that, though."

"What is it?" she says.

"I can't tell you."

Then a familiar voice fills Teurith's head.

*Teurith.*

Teurith looks toward the sky.

*Be brave, young Teurith. I will come when you call.*

"Gördög," Teurith says to herself, and her heart warms. "What's your name?"

*When needed, send for me. I am Silva.*

"Silva."

Teurith senses the Gördög flying high above her. The stone wall stretches over the fields ahead. Wrenn and Djáraad stand with their horses in front of it, talking. Teurith hears Tomas shouting at her, way behind. She doesn't care. She runs Kaspar faster, and leaps over the wall, trying to keep pace with the Gördög called Silva.

# XVI
## *Goodbyes*
### *The Year 533*

Week after week, mostly in the afternoons, Egrith and Argo meet in Grandmama's rooms, and settle in the cave-chamber beyond the wardrobe.

"I lose all sense of time when we're here," he says.

"That's the magic that lingers from Grandmama."

"It's as if time stands still."

"Sometimes when we leave we've only been gone for a few minutes." Egrith lowers her voice. "Argo?"

"Yes?"

"How did you—um—know what to do?"

"Do?"

"I never thought it would be so—lovely. I heard stories of pain, and frustration."

He reddens. "Well, I've had a little experience."

Egrith hisses her breath in and pulls away from him. "Margrin?"

"No, thank the Gods." He laughs.

"Then, who?"

"The riding master's daughter."

"But she's—"

"I know, a lot older. She knows things."

Egrith sighs. "I wish I had been your first."

"If I had, you probably wouldn't have found it to be all that pleasant. Until I was with her, I knew very little about how things worked, that a woman can feel as much, even more pleasure than a man."

Egrith blushes.

"Have you taken the Dartha Root?" he says.

"What's that?"

"It's supposed to keep women from conceiving children."

"No."

Argo frowns, and she pulls away.

"Egrith, I don't care. I will never leave you." He embraces her. "Even if, well, you— we—have a child."

"Are you in earnest?"

"I promise."

They dance.

"Will you go to the Equinox celebration tomorrow?" she says.

"Yes."

"We can't be seen together."

Argo stands still. "But after that, I go to the barracks."

"Then this is our last time for a while." She leads him to the bed of pillows in the corner, kisses him, and they lie together, bathed in the glow from the vermillion crystals.

Later, Argo kisses her, and they move into the tunnel, holding hands as they follow it upwards. They part ways after they close the door to Grandmama's chamber.

Egrith wonders when she'll be with Argo again. "Perhaps in a month or two. Oh, how long that seems," she says to herself as she dresses. She leaves her chamber and strolls through the castle, pausing to sit for a moment on a bench before going outside. She places her hand on her forehead. "Tired today." She sighs, stands and continues to an exit that leads to the large common green.

Servants set up tents in preparation for the evening's celebration. The weather is mild, the sky cloudless. Egrith watches the activity for a while, then forages in the grass along a wall. "This flower's a pretty one. But no Dartha Root." Earlier in the Hall of

Crystals she found a description of the Dartha Root, and where to look for it. She tries to stand and then sinks to the grass. "Ugh. Might lose my breakfast." She recovers and pokes around a little more, then hurries to Grena's room.

She knocks. "It's Egrith."

Margrin opens the door.

"What're you doing here?"

Margrin laughs. "I thought you'd see me if we met on neutral ground."

"I didn't have much choice, did I?" Egrith says, and flops in a chair.

"Sister of mine. I wanted to say goodbye, and talk. Just us."

"Why?"

Margrin sits by Egrith. "We haven't always gotten along, and I don't want to leave like this."

Egrith huffs. "Generous of you." Then she softens her voice. "I wish you well, Margrin."

Margrin moves closer to her sister and takes her hand. "I—I'm sorry I haven't always been very—nice." She laughs. "But you won't have to put up with me now. I'm leaving at first light."

"You seem happy, so you must really love him," Egrith says.

"Oh, I am." Margrin squeezes her sister's hand. "I wish the same for you some day, really, I do."

Egrith stays quiet.

Margrin stands and pulls her sister up, then hugs her. "I'll see you at the wedding."

Egrith tries to smile. "Yes. I look forward to it."

The door opens and Grena bustles in. "Good to see you together for once."

Egrith steps away from her sister. "Enjoy it while it lasts."

Margrin laughs again.

"Off to your chambers, both of you. Time to bathe and dress. Egrith, you look pale. Are you eating enough?"

"I'm fine, Grena. Don't worry."

Egrith returns to her rooms alone, and dresses after she washes. "Finally, this dress fits better. Guess I'm eating too much now," she says. She admires herself in the mirror, noticing how her breasts fill out the bodice of her gown. "Hmmm. Too much. At least my thighs aren't fat." She smiles, and thinks of Argo, then whispers, "I'll see you tonight from afar, my love."

Lords and ladies move through the castle on their way to the common green, dressed in bright colors; some ladies wear ribbons in their hair that trail behind them as they walk. The servants also wear their best—long flowing skirts, billowy blouses and painted leather corsets. Torches light up the green, and younger maidens dance in a circle around a pole strewn with long ribbons. A mammoth boar on a spit roasts above a fire in the center of the yard. Servants carry pitchers of wine and mead, moving through the throng as they replenish flagons.

Egrith arrives and sees her father standing with Margrin and Lord Poilet. "I guess I have to make nice. Oh, I am dizzy." She finds a fresh chalice. A servant fills it with wine, and she takes a sip. "It'll make me ill, but I don't know how else I'll get through this." She fortifies herself with another drink and approaches her father and the others.

"Hello, Egrith," the King says, and embraces her. "You look especially lovely this evening."

"Thank you, Father."

"I couldn't agree more," Lord Poilet says.

Egrith responds for Margrin's sake. "Thank you. But my sister wins the prize for the most beautiful."

"Yes. My bride-to-be is quite stunning, isn't she?" Poilet says.

"I wish you both all the happiness in the world," Egrith says, and walks away.

The evening wears on and once the boar is roasted, servants deliver platters of meat to the tables. Egrith watches Argo as he sits a few tables away with fellow soldiers of rank. "He doesn't even notice me." She pours herself more wine.

The King rises from his seat. "A toast. Please wish my daughter Princess Margrin and Lord Poilet well."

Lords and ladies stand with their cups raised.

"To Princess Margrin and Lord Poilet," the King says.

The crowd repeats, and all drink.

Egrith almost falls into her seat after the toast.

"Child, are you ill?" her father says.

"I'm alright. I just can't eat and I have a chill. May I retire soon, Father?"

"Just a little while more, then you may return to your rooms."

"Yes, Father."

Egrith turns her eyes to Argo, who isn't in his seat. She taps her foot as she surveys the green, and sees him leaning against a wall talking with one of the serving girls. Egrith stands, unsteady on her feet. She has to sit again, and then notices the girl leaves. Argo glances toward the yard and follows.

Tears roll down Egrith's cheeks before she can stop them. She rubs her eyes.

"Egrith. You may go now. I regret you do not feel well," the King says.

"I'll—be better. I just need rest." She takes his hand. "Thank you, Father."

He kisses her forehead. "Good night, Daughter."

"Good night."

Egrith drags herself through the halls. She pauses every so often to regain her balance and wipe tears from her face. At the bottom of the stairwell that leads to her chamber she has to stop, and sits on the bottom step, sobbing hard enough for her body to shake. She hears the sound of approaching footsteps and she tries to climb the stairs, but keeps tripping on the train of her dress and can't muster the energy to gather it up. As she tilts her head toward the top of the stairway, strong arms circle her from behind.

"Please let me help you," Argo says.

Egrith struggles in his arms. "You're the last person I expected to see. You must have worked fast with that serving girl."

"Egrith. That was only a ruse to keep their attention away from you and me."

"I don't believe you."

"It's true. I will never hurt you, or leave you," he says.

She relaxes in his arms and lets him help her up the stairs.

When they reach the top, he smooths hair away from her eyes, and kisses her. "What's wrong, my love? You are not well."

"Too much wine, I think."

He hugs her. "I should go. Please care for yourself, and rest. I'll try to see you when there's a break in the training. I love you, my Dearest."

"I love you as well."

Argo turns away from her and descends. Before she opens the chamber door, she watches as he disappears around the corner at the bottom of the stairwell. She pushes the door, which opens without her having to unlatch it.

She moves through the doorway.

Grena rises from a chair and Egrith runs to her arms. She lets Egrith cry and holds her until she settles herself.

"My dear girl," Grena says, and squeezes her tight. She steps back, and her eyes widen.

"What is it?"

"You're—"

"I know something's wrong with me. I'm sick, just so sick."

"No. You're not."

"Why do I feel so awful, then?" Egrith says.

"You are with child."

"How can you tell?" Egrith cries anew.

"I should have known earlier. Now I see the way you burst out of that dress, your moods, and tiredness."

"Oh, what do I do?"

"We must conceal it for as long as possible." Grena helps Egrith dress for nighttime. Egrith climbs into bed and Grena tucks her under the covers. Then she caresses her forehead. "It's Argo, isn't it?" Grena says, her voice hushed.

"Yes."

"I heard you talking. Your voices were heated."

"He'll be gone for a while now, and I won't even see him," Egrith says.

"Does he in any way mistreat you?" Grena says.

"No, never. He's good to me, and I love him."

"Perhaps your father will come around once he knows. Rest now and I will think of something."

Grena leaves.

Egrith turns on her side and faces the window, but can't sleep. As she tosses, trying to make herself comfortable, she thinks back to when she first found the secret chamber in Grandmama's rooms. "I can't rest, anyway."

She gets out of bed and moves to her armoire, where her clothes and other things are stored. Behind her riding boots she finds the green leather pouch with the gold stitching. She takes it out and sits on the edge of her bed, then removes the stone. Moonlight streams through the window and she holds the stone up in its rays until her arms tire. Then she hugs it to her, and feels it grow warm against her belly. A voice, faint at first, calls her.

"Eeee-grith."

"I'm here," she whispers, shaking.

"Don't be afraid," Grandmama says, and materializes before her.

This time, she doesn't appear in a youthful state. She looks the same as she always did to Egrith before she died.

"Grandmama, I'm so glad to see you," Egrith says, and starts to go to her.

"Be still, Child. You must listen."

Egrith stays seated on the bed.

"You are in danger," Grandmama says.

"Why?" Egrith says.

"There are those who may come for you," she says; her eyes shift to the stone and then back to Egrith. "You must be on guard."

"Who are they?"

"I cannot tell for certain. Protect the child."

"My child?"

"Yes. You will bear a child who is the hope of the Realm."

Grandmama begins to disappear.

"Wait," Egrith cries.

"Be strong, dear Egrith."

The voice of Grandmama fades and the stone grows cold.

# XVII
## *Possession*
### *The Year 549*

Grena hurries about the room and keeps the fire burning as Teurith sits nearby trying to keep warm.

"You caught a chill, that's what you did," Grena says, and adds another log. The flames crackle.

Teurith rubs her hands together to warm them.

"You shouldn't be out there in this rain. It's cold for spring."

"I have to continue my training. And I want to finish my drawing for Uncle Gareth. I used to make maps when I was home in Loring. Seems so long ago now."

"You belong in bed," Grena says.

"I'm not sick. Just cold." Teurith wraps a blanket around her shoulders, and moves to the desk by the window. She opens a drawer and takes out the piece of parchment, then spreads it on the desk. Grena looks over Teurith's shoulder at the bold strokes of black on the tan parchment, four turrets stretching into the sky, one partially eclipsed by the sun's light.

"It amazes me you're able to fashion this only using a piece of coal. But I only see the highest towers of the castle."

"In the small courtyard, the one with the towers at each corner I laid on my back in the grass just in time to see the sun passing over one of the turrets. I thought that might make a good sketch, from a beetle's eye."

"Beetle's eye?"

"Instead of bird's eye."

"Ah," Grena says.

Someone knocks.

Grena opens the door and sees King Gareth's steward.

"The King wishes to speak with you, Princess."

Teurith follows him to Reception Hall toward the main entrance of the castle. King Gareth sits on his throne. Six guards stand behind him. Teurith approaches her uncle and the steward steps in line with Lord Tannen, Djáraad and Dirk.

"Teurith," the King says.

She looks to her father; with a motion of his hand he urges her to approach the throne.

King Gareth stands. In a hushed voice, he speaks to her. "I have some news, and I am reluctant to share it lest I upset you."

"I will hear it, Uncle."

"We have Lord Magus imprisoned. My men found him in the basement of his inn at Loring, cowering like a frightened animal. He has been here for weeks, and still won't talk. He claims he doesn't remember anything that transpired while you were there months ago."

"I don't see how he doesn't. But—he wasn't himself," she says.

"If you are willing, seeing you might trigger some memory of that time for him—if he's telling the truth."

Teurith can't keep herself from shaking.

King Gareth places a gentle hand on her shoulder. "I understand if you would rather not see him."

"No, Uncle. I want to help."

"My guards and Lord Tannen will accompany us."

"My King, may I come with you?" Dirk says.

"I think it is better for you, and Teurith, if you do not."

"But—"

"My friend." King Gareth stands and places his hand on Dirk's arm. "I fear you will want Magus dead and we must question him. I will protect your daughter."

Teurith glances toward her father once before she walks with King Gareth out of the hall, followed by the guards and Lord Tannen. The door leading to the dungeon is nearby.

The King pauses, and turns to her. "Are you certain you would like to continue?"

"Yes," Teurith says.

The King nods to a guard, who takes an iron key from his belt and unlocks the door. They begin their descent and take the long stairway deep underneath the castle to the bottom, where the earthen floor is muddy. Green algae coats the rough walls on either side of the passageway. They come to another door of thick iron. The guard turns the key and the door creaks open. Two of the guardsmen move through, followed by King Gareth and Teurith, then Lord Tannen and the other guards. They pass a series of empty cells until they come to a shorter stairway that leads down.

Teurith takes the King's hand and whispers, "Did you—torture him?"

"I do not allow any forms of torture. It's barbaric, a relic from times past. Lord Magus has been confined alone in the solitary cell for weeks, and that is enough."

When they reach the bottom, they come to another passage, where two guards stand in front of the solitary cell. The King approaches them. "How is your charge today?"

"He won't take food. A bit of water, but he won't eat," the guard says, and holds the lantern up so they can see.

King Gareth stands in front of the cell where a gaunt man slumps in a corner facing away from them.

Teurith remains out of the lantern light, in the shadows where she won't be seen.

"Lord Magus," the King says.

The man doesn't respond.

King Gareth raises his voice. "Magus." The King turns to the jailor. "Open the door, then shut it behind me."

"But Sire—"

"Do as I ask."

"Yes, my King." The guard takes a ring of keys and chooses the appropriate one.

Teurith hears the lock click and moves farther into the dark.

King Gareth unsheathes his sword and approaches Lord Magus. "You, there."

Magus whimpers, and huddles against the wall.

"Get up," the King says, and prods Magus' leg with his foot.

Magus flinches.

"If you don't move, I will cut you myself."

Magus turns toward King Gareth, his hands shaking. Tears rolls through the grime that covers his face.

"Now, get up."

"Stand before your King," one of the guards says.

Magus obeys. His head droops; his hand twitches.

King Gareth lowers his sword. "You claim you don't remember anything before you came here."

"I don't remember," Magus says. Then he raises his voice. "Why am I here?"

"You are here because you allowed a young girl's life to be threatened. You are here because you and your henchmen torched an encampment of our Tinker allies," King Gareth says, and steps out of the cell. The guard closes and locks the door.

"Please, let me go," Magus whimpers.

"The clan of Tinker-folk is almost wiped out. And a young girl. You were asked to protect her, and keep her safe. You failed."

"I know nothing of that," Magus cries.

The King moves into the passageway, where Teurith waits out of sight. He whispers in her ear. "You see he is pathetic. Will you speak to him?"

"Yes. Maybe if he sees me he'll remember."

Teurith steps into Magus' view.

He shows no sign that he recognizes her.

"Lord Magus?" she says.

His eyes, vacant and glazed, stare into the space in front of her. Then, for a moment, a hint of life flickers in his eyes.

Teurith shivers.

His gaze shifts away from her and he lowers his head again.

"He doesn't see me," Teurith says, and starts to retreat into the shadows.

Then, Magus snaps his head up, his face twisted into a leer. He looks at Teurith. "Thief," a woman's voice hisses.

Teurith jumps at the sound.

"You stole from us." The shrill voice carries through the dungeon. Magus fixes his eyes on Teurith. "We are coming for you."

Magus straightens to his full height, and his scrawny form shudders. His skin bubbles, as if insects crawl under it. He collapses, then writhes on the ground. His back arches and he scuttles about upside-down on all fours, and his tongue lolls out of his mouth. Magus' strangled screams echo in the dungeon. He scampers on walls and ceiling before he finally falls to the floor in a heap.

Teurith's feet remain rooted to the ground as she watches, her eyes wild with horror.

King Gareth takes her hand. "I will see you to your chambers, Teurith. Guard, if it's not already dead, kill the creature. Make it swift and clean."

Teurith and her Uncle Gareth climb the stairs leading out of the dungeon. He doesn't let go of her hand. When the entrance is locked behind them, they walk the hallways until they come to a bench.

"Rest for a moment," he says.

Teurith sits.

King Gareth kneels in front of her and takes both of her hands in his. "You were very brave. I regret you witnessed such a terrible spectacle."

"I feel sorry for Lord Magus," she says and lowers her voice. "That wasn't him."

"No. And I have to ask. Did you recognize the woman's voice?"

"I believe so. There were three women. Then they—got younger—then turned into demon-things. The menace in Lord Magus was the same. He reminded me of them, when he—looked at me directly, and then started crawling around." She pulls her hands away and smooths the goosebumps from her arms.

"I will protect you, and my men will, Teurith. You don't have to be afraid." He hesitates. "One more question."

"Yes?"

"Why did the voice call you a thief?"

"I had to get away from those women somehow," she says. "After they—were rough with me—I grabbed the first thing I could and swung it at them, a green leather pouch with something hard in it. Then I ran away, and took it with me."

"Do you still have it?"

Teurith hangs her head. "Yes."

"It's alright. You did what you did to save yourself. Will you show me this thing?"

"I was told I should guard it with my life."

"Who told you?" he says.

Teurith rises from the bench, glances both ways down the hall, and whispers, "Queen Benadras."

"I think you had better let me see this thing for myself."

They continue through the castle to Teurith's chamber. She opens the armoire and takes the pouch out of a drawer.

King Gareth sits in the chair by the window. She stands in front of him, then removes the stone and hands it to her uncle. The rays of the setting sun make it glitter.

Teurith reaches out and touches it. "I've only used it at night and don't know if it'll work now."

"It feels like an ordinary rock, except for the smooth center."

"Yes, it's—"

"Getting warm," King Gareth says.

"That's what happens when it—shows me something, or someone."

Her uncle stands and holds the stone into the last of the sunlight. "It's hot to touch," he says.

"Uncle, let me have it."

He hands her the stone, which cools enough for her to hold it. The wall next to the window floods with light and a scene appears before them. An army marches over the plains, the sun rising to the east of them. Teurith and King Gareth see themselves riding on horseback in front of the soldiers. The scene grows more expansive and the

Barkus Wall appears ahead of the army. On the other side of the wall a horde awaits, a pink banner flying in front of them.

"That's Lord Frolichen's sigil," King Gareth says.

The stone grows cold in Teurith's hands. "That's all, I think."

King Gareth returns to the chair. "Now that I've seen something of what the stone can do, I realize you must be guarded at all times."

"I think only I can use it," she says.

"Yesterday an emissary from Incarrad City arrived. They have had famine from the drought for two years, and need grain. I negotiated with him, and in exchange for the grain they will give us gold."

"I know Incarrad City. It's north of Crispan Bay."

"That is correct. The Barkus Wall is a good halfway meeting point between Riverton and there."

"That's what the stone showed us," Teurith says.

"It's almost a three-day march south to get there. The stone revealed that you will go with us when we deliver the grain. But I am reluctant to let you. What else has the stone made apparent to you?"

"I've seen—ghosts. I saw a couple dancing in the courtyard. Djáraad said the young woman looked like me. I had never seen them before. Then, and this is horrible, a warrior charged at us, and his teeth were sharp and dripping with blood."

"I am sorry I didn't believe you, but I do now. I'll have Grena look in on you."

"Thank you," Teurith says, and hugs her uncle.

"Goodnight, Child."

"Uncle Gareth?"

"Yes, dear?"

"I have to go with you. And bring the stone. It's—important somehow."

"I must speak with your father immediately. Rest well and I'll see you upon the morrow."

# XVIII
## *The Journey*
### *The Year 533*

Egrith leans over the basin to wash her face and her stomach erupts. She makes it to the chamber pot, and loses her breakfast. "Why even bother to eat anything? Bed again." She pulls the covers over her head. Someone knocks on the door and she ignores it. "Most likely Grena." She turns over and makes herself more comfortable.

Later, the knocking returns, and wakes her. She sits up and rubs her eyes. "Come in."

Loren walks through the door. "Hello, my friend."

"Loren." Egrith tries to stand and falls back onto her bed.

"Are you ill? We've been so worried because we haven't seen you."

"I'm sorry. I haven't been feeling well," Egrith says.

"Gareth stopped by earlier and you didn't answer, so I told him I'd try this time."

"That's nice. I—" Egrith manages to get up and stumbles to the chamber pot.

Loren holds Egrith's hair back as she retches.

"What's wrong? You're sick, but why?" Loren sits on the bed next to Egrith.

"I can't tell you."

"And—you're not so thin anymore."

"I know." Egrith starts to cry.

Loren hugs her. "You can tell me. I wouldn't even tell your brother."

Egrith pulls away and wipes away her tears. "You promise?"

Grena bursts into the room.

Egrith's face darkens when she sees Grena's expression. "What's wrong?"

"Good day, Loren," Grena says, and turns to Egrith. "It's well into the afternoon. Your father wants to see you."

Loren sits in a chair and waits.

Egrith stands, stretches and kneads her lower back. "Why?"

"You've been avoiding him. And he wonders."

"Will he—notice?"

"You're so slight otherwise and that makes your belly more apparent."

"I can't go anywhere. I'm sick all day, every day."

Grena softens her tone. "I'll help you dress, and walk you to the King's chambers."

"Alright," Egrith says. "But will you please wait outside while I talk to Loren—just for a minute?"

"Yes, Child. And I'll have the healer come again later." Grena steps out the door.

"Loren, I—don't know how to speak of this."

Loren places her hand on Egrith's as they sit on the edge of the bed.

Egrith sighs. "Yes, I'm sick, but it's more than that."

Loren waits.

"I'm going to have a child," Egrith says, and lowers her head.

"But—how?"

Egrith stays quiet.

"I've never even seen you with anyone other than Argo, and that was months ago."

Egrith nods. "Mm-hmm."

"Argo?"

"Yes. I carry Argo's child."

"But you weren't supposed to have anything to do with him. How did you—"

"We had a secret meeting place."

"Please tell me how I can help you," Loren says.

"No one can help me. I must tell Father. He wants to see me, and at this point I have no choice but to tell the truth." She cries, and Loren puts an arm around her shoulder.

After a while Egrith stands. "I have to dress. Will you please stay with me until I leave?"

"I will always be here for you, dear friend."

"I know. Thank you."

Egrith washes and finds a dress with a loose bodice. She and Loren walk out the door together and find Grena waiting on the landing.

"I'm ready," Egrith says. "Loren, please come see me when you can."

"I will." Loren kisses Egrith's cheek and starts down the stairs.

Egrith turns to Grena. "I'm going to tell Father."

Grena hugs her. "You're a brave girl. I'll be there with you."

They take their time moving through the castle to King Egad's chambers. Once they arrive, they find the door open. The two guards step outside, and the King's steward says, "Princess Egrith and Grena."

Egrith moves ahead of Grena and approaches her father, who stands and embraces her. "Egrith, child. You've been ill, I hear. Has the healer been to see you?"

"Yes, he has. Father—"

"What does he tell you?"

"I am with child."

The King's face darkens, and he places a hand on his forehead.

Egrith says nothing, and tries to keep herself from trembling.

"Grena, leave us," he says.

Egrith watches Grena leave the room. She faces her father again, and shudders at his wide-eyed rage.

"There is a place I've heard of, about ten leagues from here." King Egad pauses and clenches his fists. "A man there has knowledge of certain arts that will take care of this—problem. Who is the father?"

Egrith stays quiet.

"Answer me."

She flinches.

"Is it Argo?"

Egrith's stomach roils. "Yes."

"I will have you taken to this place. This man will remove this—thing—from you."

"But Father—"

"I won't hear anything more from you." The King shakes his head. "I will banish Argo home to Martoldt Hall, where he belongs. You will never see him again."

Egrith says nothing.

"We leave immediately. I'll send for a carriage. I and my guards will accompany you." He calls his steward. "Send Grena in."

Grena enters the chamber and Egrith runs to her arms. They stand in their embrace until the King speaks again.

"Grena. Ready yourself and my daughter for a journey. We leave now."

"Sire?"

"Do not question me," the King says in a harsh voice, and dismisses them.

By the time they gather things for the journey, Egrith is calm.

They carry their bundles through the passageways until they come to the castle gate. Four armed guards escort them to the carriage then mount their horses, and two guards sit atop the carriage. King Egad arrives on his horse and taps the carriage with his riding crop. The carriage moves forward. The King and the other guards follow on horseback.

Egrith and Grena ride in silence.

As dusk approaches, Grena says in a hushed voice, "Where are we going?"

"I'm not supposed to talk about it."

Grena takes Egrith's hand and squeezes it.

Unable to sleep, Egrith stares out the window into the darkness. After a few hours, they come to the bridge that crosses the River Rys, where the King's Road becomes South Road. "There's nothing along this road," Egrith whispers to herself. "Except Mimsford, a tiny village in the midst of Lightbane Forest." She sighs and finally sleeps. Bumps in the road jar the carriage more and more as they move farther south into the forest. In the gray mist of morning, Egrith opens her eyes just as the carriage stops. She hears voices.

"Last hut on the left?"

"Last on the left," an unfamiliar voice says.

Egrith peeks out the window in time to see one of the guards toss a copper to a man on the roadside. For a moment, her eyes meet the man's gaze, and she sees fear in it. Egrith's heart thumps harder. The carriage moves ahead and she keeps her eyes fixed on the man until she can't see him anymore.

She turns to Grena. "Please. Come in with me."

"If your father doesn't restrain me I certainly will," Grena says, her voice shaky.

"You know, don't you," Egrith whispers.

"Yes, Child. I am sorry with all my heart." Grena hugs Egrith, then takes her hand again.

They continue for another mile. Dwellings become sparse, and they come to the final one. A stone wall surrounds the hut, more of a cottage made of stone and thatch. A few trees stretch their spindly arms over the yard, casting shadows on the pathway that leads to the cottage. Smoke rises from a chimney on the roof.

Egrith hears King Egad say something to his guard, who strides to the door and knocks. An old woman answers the door, her eyes glazed with a white film. Thin wisps of gray hair straggle about her face.

"What want ye? Master Arslot ain't here."

"I'll wait," the guard says.

The woman closes the door so it's ajar and she disappears. After a few minutes, she returns. "Where's the coin?"

"You'll get it when services are rendered."

"I'll have it now," she says, and cackles. "No coin, and you'll be on your way."

A man from inside the hut takes the woman's arm and shoos her away. "Can I help you?"

"You Master Arslot?"

"I am. Don't mind old Nanette. She watches over things here."

"She's blind," the guard says.

"Yes. But she sees."

Nanette shuffles over to them. "And I see more than most." She raises her voice and her eyes dart towards the carriage. "This must not happen."

"What mustn't happen?" the guard says.

"Hush, Nanette. Go back to your corner," Master Arslot says. Then he lowers his voice. "If you keep this up, I'll bind your hands again."

King Egad dismounts and dismisses the guard.

"Who are you?" Arslot says.

"That's not important. Do what you're supposed to do, then you'll get your gold."

"Very well. Where is the subject?"

The King strides to the carriage. "Come, Daughter."

Egrith obeys. With a last look at Grena she approaches the hut with her father.

Grena steps out of the carriage. "My King, may I—"

"No. Stay there."

Egrith's father guides her through the door and leaves her. She glances around the room, which is clean and neat. The old woman sits in a corner of the room, humming as she knits.

"Come here, young lady," Master Arslot says.

Egrith steps forward. A table with leather straps fastened to it stands in the center of the room. Next to that is another, smaller table with metal clamps, tongs and knives resting on it. The color drains from Egrith's face.

"Let me help you," Arslot says.

Egrith hesitates.

"It's alright. I need to see how far along you are before I begin."

She sits on the edge of the table and he helps her put her legs up, then covers her with a blanket.

Egrith trembles, and squeezes her eyes shut as the man raises the blanket, then her skirts. Someone takes her hand. She opens her eyes and sees the old woman.

"This must not happen," Old Nanette says.

"But the gold, we need it to survive," Arslot hisses. "If you interfere I'll give you a thrashing."

"If you continue, she will die, and this child must be born."

Master Arslot pulls Egrith's skirt down around her ankles, and steps away from the table. "What do I tell her father?"

"Tell him the risk is too great; she won't survive it."

Master Arslot helps Egrith down from the table and walks her to the door. Egrith looks for the woman, who has returned to her chair in the corner.

"Thank you," Egrith says.

Old Nanette doesn't respond, and continues to knit, humming softly to herself.

Egrith leaves the cottage and approaches her father.

"It can't be finished already," the King says.

"No."

King Egad storms over to Master Arslot. "What is the meaning of this?"

"If I perform the procedure, she will die."

The King says nothing, then turns to one of his guards. "Give the man ten gold pieces and prepare to depart."

King Egad takes Egrith's arm and leads her to the carriage. "Grena, I'll have words with my daughter. Leave us for now."

They step into the carriage. The King sits across from his daughter, and they sit in silence.

Finally, he speaks. "You will remain in seclusion until this child is born. You will see no one except for healers and Grena, who will bring you meals and take over the servants' duties. You will have no communication whatever with the world outside your chambers, no friends, nothing."

Egrith doesn't speak.

"Do you understand?"

"Yes," she whispers.

"And you will never see Argo again."

"Yes, Father."

The King's voice softens. "I know this is difficult for you. But you disobeyed me when I specifically told you not to see that young man. You have responsibilities to your family and the entire Realm. And now, that may all be ruined."

Egrith hangs her head.

"There, now. Try to sleep on the way home." King Egad leaves the carriage and sends for Grena.

Once Grena settles in the seat next to Egrith, she puts her arm around her shoulders. Then Egrith finally cries. The sound of the carriage wheels rolling over the uneven ground muffles Egrith's sobs. Eventually, they fall asleep together for the rest of the journey homeward.

# XIX
## *Southward*
### *The Year 549*

"There you are," Grena says. "I wanted to see you before you leave tomorrow."

"Thank you. Sweet you came by," Teurith says. She sits on the edge of the bed, and Grena moves next to her. "Grena?"

"Yes, Dear?"

"Am I old enough—to marry?"

Grena chuckles. "You're old enough from the time you begin to bleed once a month. At your age, there are struggles that come with the bleeding."

"Like what?"

"Your heart can be unstable with emotions you may not be able to control. This can be difficult for sensitive ones, like you." She lowers her voice. "And your mother." Grena places her hand on Teurith's knee.

"How old was mother when I was born?"

"She was but sixteen. Although bold and courageous, she suffered. She took everything to her heart, the sorrows of others, and all she endured."

"What happened to her?"

Grena wipes a tear from her eye. "That's a story for another time, Child. And—"

A knock on the door interrupts, and Argo's tail thumps on the floor.

"Good evening," Dirk says, enters the room and stoops to scratch the dog's head.

Grena rises from Teurith's side. "I'll be going now. Goodnight Teurith." Grena shuts the door behind her.

Dirk takes Grena's place. "Teury."

"Yes, Father?"

"Before we leave tomorrow there are things I must tell you—in case something goes awry after we deliver the grain."

"Grena was just telling me more about Mother."

He sighs. "At long last, this is the time for revealing the truth, although it pains me." He places a hand on his forehead.

"Father, what is it?"

"Teurith. First I must say I am sorry we had to keep certain things from you for so long."

Her face darkens.

"Your sweet Mother," he begins.

"How did—she die?" Teurith says.

He takes her hand. "She died of a broken heart."

Teurith waits for him to speak again.

"And I—I am not your true father."

She stays quiet for a moment, and pulls her hand away.

"Teury. You are the most important part of my life, have always been and always will be."

Teurith turns toward the window.

"Try to understand all I am about to tell you."

She faces him. "If you're not my father, then—who was?"

"Your father died in battle, the Battle of Sounding Sea Fortress. Lord Argo was your father."

"Lord Argo? Then why didn't I stay in Riverton with King Egad? Why didn't he raise me?"

"King Egad was harsh and bound by convention. He did not approve of Lord Argo, and banished him to his home at Martoldt Hall. Your mother was distraught over it. She bore Argo's child—you, Teurith. The King took you away from her, she died, and you lived in the castle for a few years in secret. Then he had me take you to Loring to raise as my own child." Dirk wipes a tear away.

Teurith lowers her head. "She died of a broken heart." She takes a deep breath and faces her father again. "But why did King Egad choose you?"

"Your mother was the only love I ever had. But I was a commoner and she later fell in love with Argo. King Egad did not approve of him—and what the King called his arrogance. And King Egad counted on making an alliance with someone else using his daughter, Egrith."

"How horrible for mother—and—Argo," Teurith cries.

"In the end, the King wanted you far away, and approached me about leaving Riverton for Loring on the condition that you remain there until your sixteenth name day."

She shakes her head slowly.

"Without her Argo, and without you to love, your Mother could not bear it." He places his arm around Teurith's shoulders.

She allows herself to cry.

Argo the dog stirs and whimpers softly, then rises and rests his chin on Teurith's knee.

"I'm sorry, so sorry. I just didn't know."

"Teury. I apologize for not being able to tell you," Dirk says.

Teurith pets Argo's head and then leans on Dirk's shoulder. "It must have been difficult for you—keeping so many secrets, losing mother, and raising me on your own."

"You are the light of my heart, and I will never regret a day raising you as my daughter."

She pulls away and sniffles.

He touches her cheek.

"Thank you for all you've done for me." Teurith embraces him.

"Try to rest, Teury. We all need it for tomorrow's journey."

Teurith climbs into bed and her father pulls the covers up around her.

"You're my father, and I love you."

He kisses her forehead. "Rest well, my dear Child."

"Goodnight." Teurith yawns and rolls on her side. She continues to cry for a while. Argo jumps on the bed and curls himself next to her. With the dog's soothing warmth, she finally sleeps.

Teurith awakens when Argo barks at the sound of knocking. She rises from bed to answer. "Father."

"It's near time to go, Teury."

"I just have to wash." She gathers her things.

"And you'll bring this stone," he says.

Teurith turns towards him. "Uncle Gareth told you."

"Yes. You were right to keep it hidden. Stay close to your uncle as you travel." Dirk hugs his daughter once more, and they leave the chamber together, Argo trailing behind.

Teurith and her father reach the King's stables, deserted now except for Kaspar. With more exercise, Kaspar is fitter and stronger than ever. Teurith mounts in her usual way, by climbing the rungs on the gate of the stall. Kaspar knows to stand still. He nickers and tosses his head.

"Good boy," Teurith says, and strokes his mane.

"Teury, remember what I said."

"If I don't stay by your wagon I'll ride with Uncle Gareth."

"Yes. All will be well."

They part and Teurith rides into the east pasture beyond the stables where the King's army prepares to march. Servants pulling carts delivering last-minute supplies for the army move through the pasture as Teurith and Kaspar search for the King. Carts bearing the grain form a line in the midst of the different battalions.

Five battalions of soldiers of three-hundred men each assemble. Lord Krimpt leads First Battalion's cavalry, Lord Tannen, the archers of Second, Djáraad, Third Battalion, and Lord Tomas leads the swordsmen of Battalion Four. The more seasoned soldiers and their leader Commander Smyth of Battalion Five bring up the rear on horseback.

Teurith finds her Uncle Gareth, who rides with his personal guardsmen and Lord Tannen. Her father sits atop a supply cart just behind the King, leading the many wagons of grain. The soldiers march behind, and narrow their formation for the march across Riverton Bridge. Teurith slows Kaspar as they cross. She waits for her uncle to finish talking with Lord Tannen.

"My two battalions from Banath Stronghold should arrive at Barkus Wall about the same time we do, perhaps a bit later," Lord Tannen says.

"I don't foresee any conflict. We'll have over two-thousand troops. That's enough to quell a skirmish," King Gareth says.

"Have you met Prince Frolichen?"

"No. We've been corresponding for years, though. He's an idealistic sort, and cares for his people. But as my father always said, he's naïve. I believe he's too willing to trust anyone who approaches him."

"Will he do as he promised? We cannot give him the grain if he doesn't provide us with the gold," Tannen says.

"He's an honorable man. True to his word," the King says.

Beyond the bridge, Lord Tannen circles around to oversee the procession of carts and soldiers, leaving King Gareth with Teurith.

"How does it feel to march with an army?" King Gareth says.

"It's glorious. And Kaspar is so proud of himself," Teurith says, and pats the horse on his neck.

"Save your strength. Three days on the march is a long time for a young girl," he says.

"This is nothing. Djáraad and I walked over rough terrain for days, and we were on the run. It's a pleasure to ride this time."

He laughs. "I know you're strong, but still."

The march continues southeast along the King's Road. Teurith stays close to her uncle or rides beside her father's wagon. The pouch with the stone is safe in a pack on her back. Her few belongings, including the jeweled chainmail shirt, are rolled into a bundle next to her father. Argo trots alongside the wagon.

"How are you doing now that it's late afternoon?" King Gareth says.

"A bit tired, I must confess." She stifles a yawn.

"We camp soon. Tomorrow we'll leave the road and head due south over the plains toward Barkus Wall."

"I think I'll rest well tonight," she says.

The King laughs again. "You deserve it."

Once off the road, King Gareth's men set up his tent. Lord Tannen sees the army off the road and the various companies make an encampment around King Gareth's tent. Teurith dismounts and takes care of Kaspar, then finds Dirk. She approaches and Argo barks, wagging his tail.

"How was the ride, Father?" She bends and scratches Argo's head.

"Easy for me. You've been on horseback all day. You must be sore," he says.

"I'm alright. Let me help you with our tent," she says.

"No need. The soldiers will pitch it. You rest. Another long day ahead tomorrow."

"I want to find Djáraad and Tomas, first."

"Don't be too long, and get some supper," her father says, and he hugs her.

As the sun sets Teurith and Argo move through the camps, searching for her friends. Soldiers laugh and sing as they rest after the day's march; some tend to pots cooking over fires.

"Hey, Lass," a man calls.

Teurith stops and glances around.

"Remember me?"

She walks to the man. "Oh, hello. Have we been acquainted?"

The old soldier laughs. "We met when you first came to Riverton. You're from Loring, and I hear a princess, niece to our King."

Teurith smiles, and approaches. "I'm just Teurith. You helped us see my uncle that day, and I thank you. May I sit?"

"And I'm just Finnan. I'd be honored."

Teurith sits on the ground next to Finnan and he hands her an apple.

She crunches into the fruit and stretches her legs out. "Do you know where I can find my friends? Third and Fourth Battalions?"

"Ah, the hatchlings. You'll have to go 'round and 'round until you bump into them. For now, enjoy a cup of hearty soup with us." He rises and stretches, then moves to the fire and pours a chunky liquid into a wooden bowl. Finnan stoops as he walks, favoring his right foot.

"Are you injured?" Teurith says as he hands her a bowl.

"Oh, that's just the stiffness from being on the horse all day."

"But, your foot," she says.

"It's an old battle injury, from the time of your grandfather, King Egad."

"You were in the Battle of Sounding Sea Fortress?"

"Yes. It was long, and hard. Better not to speak of it now." Finnan slurps from his bowl as Argo stares and licks his chops.

Teurith finishes and stands. "Thank you, Finnan. I hope we meet again soon."

"Yes indeed, Lass. We shall."

Teurith circles the encampment until she hears Djáraad's voice. "Teurith. Here." Argo barks, runs ahead and she follows.

"I was going to come find you," he says. "Take your pack off and stay a while."

"Pack stays on," she says, in a hushed voice.

"Of course. Come. It's quiet in here." He opens the flap of his tent and they move through the opening. "I'd rather sleep under the stars with my troops but all commanders have tents to themselves. I just had a meeting with the other leaders."

"How did that go?" Teurith says, and plops on a cushion.

"It was strange. I didn't say much. Although this march is more of a training mission for the soldiers, Lord Krimpt lectured us about maintaining formation and staying at the ready, always protecting the King. And you."

Teurith says, "Does he know about—"

"No. As long as you stay close to your uncle, you'll be safe." He lowers his voice. "And the stone will, too." He lights a lantern.

"I thought for sure Tomas would be here."

"He's with his men, has his own tent."

"Lord Krimpt is fortunate to have you and Tomas. Some of these recruits, especially the nobles, are louts," she says.

"If it actually came to battle, they'd throw their lives on the line for you."

"That may be. It's you two I worry for. Would they do the same for you?" She shifts her position. "Tomas seems awfully grim of late. What's disturbing him?"

"I—can't give him what he wants."

"What do you mean?"

"In our tribe, we have love in many forms. It's acceptable for a man to take a husband, and a woman to take a wife. While Tomas is my friend and I respect him, I cannot return his—affections."

"You're saying Tomas—"

"He wants our comradery to move beyond what I can give him. And I can't because—I love another."

"No wonder he's angry with his sister. You mean to court Wrenn? She's—"

"Not Wrenn," Djáraad says, and stands. "I—"

"Hello?" Teurith jumps up.

"What's wrong?"

"The stone. It's getting hot."

# XX
## *Demands*
### *The Year 533*

Egrith sits by the window, a blanket thrown over her legs. She raises herself from the chair, clutching her swollen belly and her lower back.

"Oh, you're there," she says, as the baby kicks within her. "At least I have you."

She looks out the window at the view over Riverton. "Lonely." She sighs. "And hungry. Grena should be here soon."

She paces. "Legs ache. Have to walk in spite of." The baby kicks again and she allows herself to smile. Soon Grena knocks, and Egrith moves to the door.

"Dear Grena, thank you."

Grena places a tray of food on the table. "It's those dumplings you like so much. Try and eat the meat, too. You need your strength for the child."

"Yes. He's been active today."

"She," Grena says.

"How do you know?"

"I just do." She laughs.

"It feels like a boy. Come, touch my stomach, and you'll know it's a him."

Grena hugs Egrith and places a hand on her belly. "Good. You seem better, stronger now."

"Wait a moment...there. Did you feel that?"

"She's a kicker for sure. How are you—apart from the child?"

"I miss Loren. And Dirk. And my brother. And—"

"Hush, now. It is better for Argo to be home at Martoldt Hall, away from the King's wrath."

"I love you, Grena, but I haven't seen anyone else for months. Has Father softened any?"

"I cannot say." Grena lowers her voice. "He means to visit you."

"Why? He hasn't been here in all this time. He's punishing me," Egrith says.

"Perhaps he has had time to think, and will accept you—and the child."

Egrith sniffles. "I can only hope."

Grena touches her cheek. "I must go. I'll look in on you later."

Egrith watches Grena open the door and close it behind her.

The sun sets and Egrith tires. She pulls the covers back, climbs in bed and sleeps. When she awakens it's dark in her chamber, and someone knocks at the door. "Just a moment." She finds a candle, lights it and answers the door. Grena stands before her and shoos her inside.

"Hurry. You must dress. Your father approaches."

Egrith washes, pulls a dress over her shift and brushes her hair.

Another knock, and Grena opens the door for the King.

"Leave us," he says.

Grena obeys with a fleeting glance at Egrith, who faces her father.

"Come, Child." He embraces her.

Egrith sobs in his arms.

"There, there." He caresses her hair and places his hands on her shoulders. "I am sorry, my Daughter. Sorry for the way I treated you. I do not want to lose you. As I have lost Margrin."

"Margrin? What happened?" Egrith says.

"She has been taken. Forces from the south surrounded Sounding Sea Fortress with threats. Lord Poilet has betrayed us. He gave Margrin up in exchange for their protection."

"How horrible. What will you do? We can't let them have her."

"I have ordered my army to assemble. We will fight for her."

"I thought the Realm was at peace. Are your troops prepared for wartime?"

"Do not fret. We will take Sounding Sea Fortress and rescue your sister. Lord Poilet will pay for his spineless transgression."

King Egad paces.

"I am sorry, Father."

"I wanted to see you before I leave tomorrow. I need you to live, be free and happy."

"Free?"

"About this child. Grena reports you are healthy, as is the baby." King Egad looks away for a moment.

"Father?"

"After its birth, the wet nurse will take it; someone far away will raise it. You will have no part after."

"How can you do this?" Egrith cries. "The child has done you no harm. It isn't fair."

"There is still hope you might marry and cement an important alliance. No one knows of this. The court believes you are sick, and confined to your rooms for that reason alone."

"But—"

He raises his voice. "We will speak of this no further." After a moment, he takes her hand. "Try to rest, Egrith. You'll bear the child and that is all, nothing beyond."

The King leaves.

Egrith lowers herself on the chair and stares out the window into the night, tears streaming down her cheeks. "I can do nothing, nothing," she whispers, and feels the child kick again. "I only have you. For now."

Weeks pass. Egrith remains in bed more and more, the baby heavy on her thin frame. She sees Grena at mealtimes, and doesn't eat much.

"You need to nourish yourself," Grena says, and brings a cup of broth to Egrith, who stays under the covers. Grena sits on the edge of the bed, and dips a crust of bread in the hot liquid. "Have this."

Egrith tries to lift her head, and then lets it rest on the pillow again. "Maybe tomorrow," she says. "Grena?"

"Yes, my Dear?"

"Is there news from Father?"

"None I am supposed to give you. I will say, they are trying to negotiate for your sister's safe return."

"Will there be war?"

"Try to at least rest if you can't eat." Grena leaves the broth and bread on the table. "I'll stay with you until you sleep." She kisses Egrith's forehead.

Long before dawn Egrith wakes, her body drenched with sweat. She sits up, and squints into the darkness. "Grena?" She moves her legs over the side of the bed, stands and approaches the table, lifts the mug and sniffs at the broth. "Ugh." She puts it down and sits by the window. The child stays quiet in her belly. "You must be asleep." She sighs, and thinks of the green leather pouch stitched with gold trim that holds the stone. "If I could only see Grandmama again." Her head droops with fatigue.

A rustling sound startles her, and she snaps her eyes open. Her sight, now adjusted to the dark, lets her scan the chamber. "Must be imagining things." She shifts her position in the chair, pulls the blanket tighter around her, closes her eyes again, then sleeps.

*A young girl races through a meadow, a mammoth dog bounding along by her side. The girl stops, then bends to stroke the dog's fur. He wags his tail so fiercely his entire back end wiggles, and she laughs. They continue loping through the fields of high grass and wildflowers.*

Egrith's eyes open. "What a lovely dream." She yawns and stretches. As she starts to rise from the chair so she can return to bed, a pale green light fills the room, faint at first, then becoming more present.

Fear floods her stomach. She feels the child stir.

Wind blows the drapes on the windows and rattles the furniture, then forms a whirlwind. The vortex grows larger, twisting about the chamber, which is bathed in the dirty, green light. The whirlwind pauses in the center of the room. Flashes of light blind Egrith and she stumbles towards the bed. The chamber rumbles. She closes her eyes and holds her hands over her ears, a high-pitched, sustained tone assaulting them.

Then, all is quiet.

Egrith hesitates before she opens her eyes again. When she does, three women stand in front of her. Her eyes widen.

The tallest woman, who stands between the two others, takes a step toward Egrith. Egrith flinches. "Who—who are you?"

The woman's black eyes ignite with menace, and her blond hair blows about her face. "Where is the artifact?"

"Artifact?"

"Give it to us or we shall cut this child from your womb and leave you to die."

Egrith shudders, and then her nerves steady. "I have nothing of yours. Leave. I'll call the guards." She opens her mouth to shout, then her throat constricts and she can't speak at all.

"If you give us the stone, you will survive. If not, you will perish and we will take your child."

Then Egrith understands. Her Grandmama said to keep the stone hidden, and safe. But she fears for her child. Her heart flutters, and she tries to stand, then falls to the bed.

"Hurry. Give us the artifact, now." The woman lunges at Egrith and begins to shake her.

"Please, stop," Egrith whimpers, and tries to break free of the woman's hold.

"Now."

"Alright."

The woman releases Egrith.

Egrith rises and moves toward the wardrobe. She opens the door and finds the pouch, hidden behind her riding boots.

"Give it to me."

Egrith obeys.

The three women move together in a huddle and hiss at one another. They raise their arms toward the ceiling and another vortex swirls around them. The noise from the whirlwind grows louder until Egrith screams from the pain in her ears. A shrill, green light blinds her. Then the twister disappears, leaving the room in silence.

Egrith leans against the wall, her voice choked with sobs. "Guards," she whispers, and feel a dampness soaking her shift. "Guards," she says, louder.

The door bursts open.

"Fetch Grena and the midwife," Egrith says before she collapses.

"...and she'll wake again soon. Then the pains will come," Grena says.

Egrith opens her eyes and finds herself lying in her bed with a compress on her forehead.

"My dear girl, how do you feel?"

"The baby's coming."

"A bit too early, but yes, anytime now."

Pain stabs Egrith, and she tries to sit up. "But what if—"

"Lie still," Grena says, and whispers something to another woman in the room, who must be the midwife, Eni.

"There's naught I can give her for pain," Eni says. "I have some ointment to rub on her legs and stomach. That should relax her."

Grena turns to Egrith, and begins to rub the oil on her. "You must be brave. Try to relax and lie still. We will help you."

Egrith sighs, and starts to shut her eyes.

"Stay awake," Eni says. "You mustn't sleep."

Egrith's eyes flutter, then shut. She frowns and her head moves from side to side.

"Try and roust her, whilst I prepare a basin. There will be much blood. She's not far enough along yet," Eni says, and brings the basin next to the bed. She pulls down the coverlet.

Egrith cries out, and her arms flail and grasp at nothing.

"We'll have to restrain her. She's not altogether with us," Eni says. "Go and find something to bind..."

*Egrith laughs, and the young girl takes her hand and pulls her through the field of wildflowers. They see someone ahead, and the girl drops Egrith's hand and runs toward the figure. "Father," she says, and the flowers almost swallow her as she races forward. Egrith follows. They run toward him and into his embrace. "My loves," he says. "Argo," Egrith says. They stroll together through the field toward the setting sun and—*

"…nothing else I can do and we're losing her," Eni says.

Egrith opens her eyes, frantic, and she glances around her. "I can't move."

Grena bends over her. "You're here. Thank the Gods. You were thrashing about. We had to tie your arms. How—"

Egrith screams.

"The contractions are getting closer. The child is coming. Push, Princess!" Eni says.

Egrith fights the urge to sleep and pushes.

"More, Child," Grena says, as the midwife waits at the foot of the bed.

Egrith wails, the sound of her screams filling the chamber.

Eni bends forward as the sound of a baby's crying eclipses Egrith's screams.

Egrith shudders, then becomes still. "My child," she says.

After a few moments, Grena steps to her holding a bundle. "Egrith, dear, your daughter." She places another pillow behind Egrith's head and helps her sit up. Grena hands her the baby.

Egrith gazes at her daughter, and kisses her on the top of her head. "How lovely. I shall call you—Teurith."

"A beautiful name," Grena says.

Someone knocks.

"Please, wait a minute," Grena says.

The knocking persists.

Egrith's eyes widen. She holds Teurith to her breast, and the child begins to cry. "No," Egrith says.

"My dear, they have come," Grena says.

"No," Egrith cries. "Just a few hours, please."

"I am sorry, Egrith. I must obey the King. You—"

"Gods, please, no," Egrith says, her words strangled with sobs, and baby Teurith cries harder.

"Open the door," a guard says.

Eni moves to the door and opens it.

One of the guards escorts another woman into the room, who moves towards Egrith.

"You cannot take her from me," Egrith says.

"King's orders. Please, Lass. I don't want to force you—" the guard says.

"No," Egrith shouts, as she holds the child closer.

The woman, plump and stern, pries Egrith's hands off Teurith, and takes the screaming child. The guard holds Egrith's wrists as she kicks and writhes.

"No, no, no," Egrith whimpers as the door shuts.

"There, now. It's for the best," Grena says.

"Better not to have made the child at all," Eni says.

"Hold your tongue, Eni. You're dismissed." Grena sits on the bed by Egrith, who shakes with sobs. Grena smooths away the sweaty hair from Egrith's face. "I'll stay with you. As long as you want."

Egrith stops crying. "I want to be by myself. You can go, Grena. I am alone. From now on."

# XXI
## *Reaching Barkus Wall*
### *The Year 549*

Djáraad moves to the entrance of the tent and secures the flap. The lantern grows dimmer and burns out. They are left with only the sound of Argo snoring nearby.

In the darkness, Teurith removes the stone from her pack. It glows and gives off a pale blue light. Djáraad sits on a cushion next to her as the tent becomes brighter. A dancing couple, like the time in the castle courtyard, materializes.

The stone widens as the image of the couple becomes more present, then life-sized. They continue to dance, Teurith and Djáraad watching them from the cushions.

"Mother—and father," she whispers.

The couple stops. Teurith's father, Argo, bows to her mother, Egrith, and she curtsies, then turns toward Teurith.

"She sees me," Teurith says.

Egrith blows her a kiss and smiles, then she fades into darkness.

"Look," Djáraad says, as Argo steps forward, and bows again.

"Teurith, my sweet Daughter," Argo says, his brow furrowed. "Please, help us."

"Help you?"

Argo's face relaxes. He smiles, then the corners of his mouth turn down again. "I love you, my dear Daughter, and your mother, sweet Egrith."

Djáraad starts to speak and Teurith places her hand on his arm to stop him.

"Dirk was my friend. He also loved your mother, and has been a good father to you."

"Yes," Teurith says, and a tear rolls down her cheek.

"You are the hope of the Realm, and always have been."

"I'm just a child."

"I must leave you now. Be brave, my daughter." The ghost of Argo fades and the tent darkens.

Djáraad stands and lights the lantern. "Your father?"

"Yes." Teurith rises and he takes her in his arms.

Teurith hugs Djáraad and rests her head on his chest. As she becomes aware of his body against hers she pulls away. "Um," she says, and clears her throat. "I'm—confused."

"About your parents?" he says.

"No. I haven't had a chance to tell you. Father—Dirk the Blacksmith—told me of my true father—Lord Argo—before we left to march south." She hesitates.

"What is it?"

Teurith opens the tent flap, pokes her head out and looks around. Then she secures the flap again. "I don't understand how I can help anyone, much less the entire Realm. Did Argo—mean save the Realm sooner or later?"

"He didn't say how or when."

"Maybe when I'm older. For now, I have to be prepared." She returns to the cushions. "I think we need another look."

"In the stone?"

"Yes." Teurith takes the stone out and holds it in her lap. Noise from outside the tent, sounds of soldiers singing and talking, fades as the lantern flickers and brightens. The stone heats up again.

"Something's happening," she says.

The scene shifts, and a warm breeze blows around them.

"What's that smell?" Teurith says, and a gray sky appears above.

"I've only seen the Sounding Sea once but I'll never forget the salty smell," Djáraad says.

They feel soft sand under them, and see the ocean beyond. Gulls screech overhead and they hear the sound of many feet tramping. Teurith stands first, then Djáraad.

Forms of soldiers appear and move past them, some carrying weapons, others leading their horses.

"It's an army. I hear them marching, but they—they're gliding, not walking," Teurith says.

"They're ghosts," Djáraad says, and takes her hand.

A voice carries over the wind. "Teurith."

She drops Djáraad's hand. "I don't recognize the voice." She gazes at the ghosts; one of them floats toward her. Teurith's knees weaken and she trembles.

The phantom soldier speaks. "Teurith. We will answer your call."

She hesitates. "You're a spirit."

"Yes. We are The Fallen, and wander the earth until we are needed."

"The Fallen?"

"We are soldiers who were slain in battle by those who seek to destroy all that is good in the Realm. We wander until needed by those who are true of heart."

"If I am to summon you, then when?"

"You will know the time." The ghost-soldier fades.

"Wait, can you tell me more?"

The sound of soldiers marching diminishes until all is quiet. Teurith and Djáraad stand and gaze at the sea; a flash brightens the sky and their surroundings blur.

"We're in the tent again," Teurith whispers, and Argo the dog whines and licks her hand.

Djáraad pets Argo, and the dog wags his tail. "It's late. I'll walk you back."

Teurith returns the stone to her rucksack. "I'm not going to talk about it."

"About the ghost army?" Djáraad says.

"That, too. I mean—about Lord Argo. Father—Dirk—raised me as his own. I love him dearly, and he has always been good to me."

Djáraad stops walking. "You're remarkable."

She faces him. "So are you."

The sun sets. They continue moving through the encampment, pausing from time to time to talk with soldiers from the different battalions. They reach Dirk's tent, where he sits on the ground in front of it, smoke from his pipe curling in wisps above his head. Argo stretches and sits by Dirk's side.

"Father," Teurith says.

He stands and she hugs him.

"What's that for?" Dirk says, and laughs.

"Just because I love you."

"And I love you, Teury."

At first light, the troops start packing in preparation for the second day of the march. Teurith wakes before Dirk, and watches him sleep. She smiles, and rises to wash and dress. Her stomach growls and she steps outside to look for breakfast. The guards stationed around King Gareth's tent talk with one another as they break camp.

"Good morning. Any breakfast left?" Teurith says to one of the guards.

"The King's just having his. Go ahead in," he says.

Teurith walks through the entrance of the tent and sees her uncle.

"Well, Teurith. Have something to eat with me," King Gareth says. "Please, sit."

She sits on a cushion next to her uncle. "Father was still asleep. May I take him some breakfast after we finish?"

"Certainly. It's more of the same. Potatoes with bits of beef and vegetables—thick and hearty. The march will be more difficult today without the good road beneath us."

"It's not that far to Barkus Wall, though," she says.

"No. Just more uneven terrain. We'll have to move slower for the carts. And there's an uphill climb at the end."

Teurith eats her soup and says, "Uncle?"

"Yes, Dear?"

"Can you tell me about the Battle of Sounding Sea Fortress?"

His brow furrows. "You are right to ask. Not much has been documented about it. King Egad—my father—did not make decisions that were for the good of everyone. He—"

A guard enters the tent. "My King, a rider."

"Excuse me, Teury, I must see about this."

Teurith carries a bowl of breakfast to Dirk's tent. He steps out as she arrives.

"Father, there's a rider to see Uncle Gareth."

He frowns. "Not necessarily a concern. But today, wear your chainmail shirt under your leathers. We should reach Barkus Wall by nightfall. Keep it on until we're on our way home to Riverton."

"Yes, Father." She gathers her things and pulls the chainmail shirt over her head. "And now the stone." She loops her arms through the straps on her rucksack. "Time to fetch Kaspar." She moves to where the horses are tied and finds her father talking to King Gareth, already sitting his warhorse.

"…should ride on the cart with you today. She looks tired."

"Yes, my King," Dirk says and sees his daughter. "Oh, Teury."

"Father, please let me ride Kaspar again. I'm not tired, and I—"

King Gareth says, "Ride with your father. I feel something's not right and want you safe."

"Is it because of that rider?"

The King considers. "No. I am simply ill at ease."

Teurith hesitates and says, "Very well, Uncle. Kaspar will know to ride alongside us." She climbs on the cart next to her father; Argo jumps up and stretches out at their feet.

The battalions move into formation alongside and behind the procession of carts. King Gareth, Lord Tannen and the King's guardsmen lead.

"Father?"

"Yes, Teury," he says.

"Did Uncle Gareth tell you about the rider?"

"It wasn't dire news. Lord Frolichen sent word that he is already camped at Barkus Wall. He had his men knock down a small portion of the wall so the carts could freely pass. That seems harmless enough, but I know the King worries."

"Has Barkus Wall ever been breached? I've heard there are places where it's crumbling, but never knocked down." She lets Argo drink from her water pouch.

Her father smiles, and gazes at the horizon.

"You're sad?" Teurith says.

"I was thinking of your mother."

"What about her?"

He sighs. "One day, many years ago, four friends rode near Barkus Wall, on the edge of Lightbane Forest."

"That's where the wall is lower, isn't it?"

"Yes. On a dare, your mother raced the warhorse called Kraken and jumped the wall. My horse stopped short of it and I was thrown. She was the bravest of all of us."

"Was Uncle Gareth there?"

"Yes. And your father, Argo."

Teurith stays quiet.

Hills roll under them as the day wears on, and the march slows even more. After a few hours of negotiating hilly terrain, the sun starts to set.

"It'll be nightfall well before we're camped. No wandering about tonight. Stay close," Dirk says. "Now we begin going up."

A gradual ascent looms in front of them. The light of the sun fades as they travel slower, the procession of carts and army moving uphill.

"The sun's gone. What's that glow?" Teurith says.

"It can only be campfires from Lord Frolichen's army," her father says.

"We're close, then."

"Too close, I fear."

After another hour, a guard circles around to Dirk's wagon. "The King says to stay with your daughter and the cart once we arrive. We'll assemble men to surround your tent."

Horsemen approach and ride along with Dirk and Teurith. They finally reach the crest of the hill. Dirk hisses his breath in. The valley below flickers with a myriad of campfires.

"Gods, why so many?" Teurith says, her voice hushed.

"Something's not right."

"But—"

"Quiet, now."

Gradually, the carts of grain and battalions of soldiers finish their ascent and make camp. Lord Tannen rides to Dirk's cart and dismounts. "Dirk, you and Teurith will stay with the King in his tent where you'll be guarded properly. We'll take care of the wagon. Go, now."

Teurith grabs her bedroll and glances at her father, who helps her step from the cart. Argo follows them to the King's tent.

"…be ten-thousand strong. And my troops from Banath are nowhere to be seen," Lord Tannen says.

"They may not let a messenger pass; no sense sending a rider west," King Gareth says, and turns to Dirk. "Good. You're here. I think—"

One of the guards pokes his head in. "My King?"

King Gareth moves outside. After a few moments he returns and takes Dirk aside, although Teurith still hears what he says.

"Lord Frolichen's emissary said he requests a meeting. Right now. I told him I'd ride out in the morning."

"Why?" Dirk says, with a glance at Teurith.

"This is a trap, I know that much. I must decide how to proceed. For now, encourage Teury to rest, and get some yourself."

The King and Lord Tannen leave the tent again as Dirk and Teurith settle down.

"Father," Teurith whispers.

"Hush, Teury. Try to sleep."

Teurith puts an arm around Argo and he sighs. His warmth soothes her, and after a long while of staring at the ceiling of the tent, she closes her eyes.

*…drums beat in the distance, the sound carrying through a dense fog. The pulse of the beating is steady, but off-kilter, in groups of odd numbers. BUM-bum BUM-bum-bum BUM-bum. BUM-bum BUM-bum-bum BUM-bum. Over and over it repeats, until the sound lets her think of nothing else. Then another sound emerges, the pounding of spears on the ground in a steady rhythm. Then the chanting starts. The name FANG-thar repeats with every pound of a multitude of spears, in a grotesque counterpoint to the drumming. The fog lifts and a legion of soldiers moves towards her. They don't have to move fast. Teurith is alone with nowhere to go. With chants of FANG-thar growing louder, a rider flanked by two banner carriers threads his way through the throng of soldiers. The banner is red with the head of a demon stitched in the center. Fear spreads through her entire being. When the rider almost reaches her, he stops. Teurith's knees quiver, but she stands her ground. He removes his red-plumed helmet. Then he smiles, and she screams…*

"The Teeth, The Teeth," Teurith says, as Dirk shakes her awake.

"Teury, just a dream," he says. "You're very pale. Here, take some water and eat this." He hands her a flask, a bit of dried beef and a pear.

She sits up and glances around. "Where is my Uncle?"

"He's been with Lord Tannen and his advisors through the night. We must remain alert. I am sorry you didn't rest well but we have to prepare ourselves."

They finish eating, roll their blankets and wait just outside the tent. The soldiers stand ready, spread out over the hilltop. Just as the sun appears on the horizon, King Gareth arrives.

"Let's talk inside," the King says.

Dirk and Teurith follow him into the tent.

King Gareth kneels in front of Teurith, and takes her hands in his. "Teurith. Things are not what they should be. I must ride out to meet Lord Frolichen. I am allowed but two guards. If I for some reason do not return, you, with the help of your father and my advisors, will rule in my stead. You are next in line."

"But, Uncle, I—"

"Do not worry. You will have the help you need when the time comes. You are the hope of the Realm."

"Uncle Gareth, please, don't go. Can't you send someone else?"

"No. Be brave, dear girl." He leaves.

Teurith starts to follow and Dirk takes her arm.

"No, father. I want to see what happens." She kisses his cheek and moves the flap of the tent aside, then walks outside into the morning light with Argo.

Teurith waits on the hill and sees carts of grain already filing through the opening in the wall. A tent with pink banners flying above it stands at the bottom of the hill beyond the wall, surrounded by soldiers. The form of King Gareth grows smaller as he rides towards the tent with his two guards.

Teurith hears the sound of hoof beats.

Lord Tannen trots towards her. He dismounts. "Teurith. I have instructions from the King for you and your father. If something goes awry you will ride with a small company from Third Battalion as fast as you can back to Riverton."

She stays quiet, and thinks of Djáraad and Tomas.

"The King is with Lord Frolichen by now."

"Yes," she says.

After about an hour King Gareth and his guards start up the hill, riding towards them. Teurith trembles with excitement. "Uncle Gareth," she says. "He's coming back, Lord Tannen. Maybe all's well and we can go home."

Tannen places a hand on her shoulder. "We'll see, young Teurith."

She keeps herself from running to meet them. The King's guards take his warhorse after he arrives and dismounts. "Come, Teury. We hold council now. I want you with us."

Commanders from the five battalions and their companies already wait in the council tent when King Gareth, Teurith and Dirk, and Lord Tannen arrive. Teurith sees Djáraad and Tomas among them.

King Gareth addresses everyone. "If we leave now, without the gold Lord Frolichen promised, they will not hinder us. But there's a complication. They have two hostages.

If we surrender half of our troops they will return these hostages, and we may retreat to Riverton."

Lord Tannen speaks. "Who are they holding?"

"It is difficult for me to believe, and I won't until I see for myself." The King hesitates. "They apparently have my sister Margrin—and her son."

"But Margrin is dead," Dirk says.

"That is what we've always been led to believe."

Teurith steps forward. "But you can't surrender our men—you just can't."

"What else am I to do?" the King says.

Teurith glances at Djáraad and their eyes meet.

She steps forward. "The Gördög, Silva, and the ghost army can help us."

All eyes turn towards Teurith.

She removes the stone from her rucksack.

"Teurith," her father cries.

"The time has come," she says. "It has been revealed to me that I must use the stone when it is most necessary. With this stone and help from Silva and the army of The Fallen, we may defeat our enemy."

Djáraad moves next to Teurith. "It's true. All of it. We may have a chance. I would have us wait until we have Margrin and her son, then attack. They will believe we have only two-thousand troops. It might be worth the risk."

King Gareth considers. The various leaders murmur among themselves, and a guard enters the tent. "Sire, the carts of grain are through."

The King nods. "Commanders. Prepare your men. Arrows at the ready. No one lets them fly until we have Margrin. Teurith, stay here with your father. I'll send for you when you're needed."

Teurith and Dirk wait.

In Teurith's mind, she calls the Gördög. *Silva.* The other encounters she's had with Silva have been spontaneous. This time, she has to summon her. *Silva.* The Gördög could be anywhere, and may not arrive in time. Teurith focuses her thoughts and calls out to Silva over and over.

King Gareth returns. "We have Margrin. And her son. The boy is sickly. Margrin— is broken. Teurith, we must act soon."

"I'm trying, Uncle, but—"

A guard shouts, "My King, they're attacking."

King Gareth runs from the tent after a last glance at Teurith. She follows him out before her father can stop her.

# XXII
## *Relief*
### *The Year 533*

Day after day, Egrith remains in bed. Grena encourages her to eat and drink water, spoon-feeding her bits and drops at a time. After two weeks, as Grena pulls the curtains aside and opens the window, Egrith speaks.

"Grena." Her voice is raspy, and she's short of breath.

"Yes, my Dear."

"What news?"

Grena sits, and takes her hand. "Loren has been asking for you. With the King still away, I see no reason why she can't visit."

"Have you heard anything—about Margrin?"

Grena squeezes her hand and looks away.

"What's wrong?" Egrith says, and tries to lift her head.

"Child, your sister has disappeared and is presumed dead."

"How horrible—poor Margrin," she says, and adjusts her pillow. "Then we lost the war."

"No. The King was able to push the forces from the south back and take Sounding Sea Fortress. Lord Poilet remains imprisoned there for betraying us."

"Horrid man. Oh, my sister, I wish we had been closer," Egrith cries.

"None of this is your fault. There is always discord between sisters. Send her your love."

"But—"

"There, now. Try to rest again," Grena says and caresses Egrith's cheek.

Grena leaves and Egrith tries to stand. She's thinner now, except her breasts still weigh her down. "Oh, my child. If only I had you, maybe I could keep going without Argo." She cries and moves to the chair by the window. She looks out over the town of Riverton. West of her tower, she imagines she sees Smithy Lane, and thinks of Dirk. "Seems so long ago. Wish we could all be friends again, like when we were younger." She sighs and watches the activity below. "I should feel grateful. At least I can be miserable in comfort."

But she isn't comfortable. In the pit of her stomach, a heaviness forms a knot. "It's the dread feeling again." She rubs her belly to try and smooth the anguish away. "Where the child was, is now filled with sorrow. And it's in my head, too. No hope."

Egrith buries herself under the covers. Exhausted from burdens of loss—she sleeps. When she opens her eyes again, the chamber is dark. She turns her body and faces the other way, toward the window. As she falls asleep, she hears something, and props herself up on her elbows. The sound of a baby wailing, faint at first, comes from the window. She gets out of bed, draws the drapes aside and opens it, then leans out as far as she can. "Where are you?" The crying stops. A dizzy sensation overwhelms her and she pulls herself in before she loses her balance. She gathers her strength and falls into bed.

She wakes in the dawn, shivering, and pulls the coverlet up around her face. Grena returns later, and rushes toward the window. "Gods, Child. You'll catch your death." A cold wind blows the heavy drapes about. Grena gathers them and shuts the window. "Let's get you washed and dressed today." She helps Egrith out of bed and finds a dress of plush blue velvet with long sleeves.

"Thank you, Grena. This dress feels lovely, soft and warm. Why is it so cold?" Egrith says. Her teeth chatter.

"Storms coming, I think." Grena uncovers the breakfast platter. "Have some cheese and bread. You need some nourishment so the chill will leave you."

Egrith takes a sip of water and nibbles at a piece of cheese.

"Good girl. I'll return later with your supper." She kisses Egrith's cheek and leaves the chamber.

The day stays dark and cold with the coming storm. Egrith opens the window a crack and sees angry clouds loom in the distance. She wraps a blanket around her shoulders and watches lightening flash on the horizon as the storm approaches. By midafternoon rain pelts the window sideways, and she finally closes it. She dozes until someone knocks. "Must be Grena again. Come in." She yawns.

Loren steps into the chamber.

Egrith rises too quickly and has to plop in the chair again.

"Oh, don't get up. I'll pull a chair by you," Loren says, and stoops to hug her friend.

Egrith smiles. "I'm so happy to see you."

"Yes. Me, too. It's been so long." Loren sits by Egrith.

"How have you been feeling? You have your ailments as well."

"Stairs are difficult. But I try to walk about the castle and that relieves some of the pain in my joints," Loren says.

"Moving around is good for you." Egrith lowers her head. "I haven't left this room for months."

"I'm so sorry. That was insensitive of me. Now that—you've had the child—surely you're free to come and go as you please."

Egrith sighs. "Now I don't even want to leave the chamber." She grasps Loren's arm. "Have you heard anything—about my daughter?"

"No, not even rumors. I didn't even know the baby was a girl. I am sorry, Egrith," Loren says with tears in her eyes.

"Thank you. I'll be sorry forever."

They both stand and embrace. Loren holds Egrith until she stops crying. "I'll come again tomorrow, if that's alright."

"I would like that," Egrith says, and walks Loren to the door.

Egrith tires and returns to bed, the pouring rain loud in her ears. Thunder rumbles as the storm gets closer. With her stomach roiling, she tries to sleep but can't, and then she hears a knocking. This time, she gets out of bed and answers the door.

Her spirits soar as her brother Gareth stands before her. She takes his hand and pulls him into the chamber. He picks her up and spins her around. After he sets her down, they hug for a long time.

"My dear Sister. Loren told me—about the child. Father was wrong, so wrong, about everything."

"What's done is done. I will have to live with that." She sighs and wipes tears from her eyes. "I'm so glad you're safe. And Father?"

Gareth frowns, and he looks toward the window.

"What's wrong, was Father hurt? Is he—"

"Our father is well, a small wound on his leg, nothing serious. That wouldn't have been the case if—"

"If what?" Egrith says, as lightning flashes in the chamber.

"Father is only alive because Argo saved him."

"Argo? But he—he's home at Martoldt Hall."

Gareth shakes his head, and takes her hand.

"What happened?"

"We were losing the battle, without hope, without enough forces. Argo arrived with a thousand fresh troops. He fought with valor, and threw himself into the melee. Our father's horse took a spear in the side and he was left to fight hand-to-hand. I couldn't get to him. Argo broke through the enemy's circle surrounding Father and saved him."

"Then Father will certainly forgive him and allow him back at court," Egrith says, her heart fluttering with joy.

Gareth embraces her again.

She pulls away. "But—where is Argo now?"

He stays quiet.

"Tell me, Gareth." Her face drains of color as a peal of thunder cracks overhead.

"Our Father is alive because of Argo's bravery, but Argo fell—with a mortal wound."

"No," Egrith whispers. She collapses in her brother's arms, and sobs.

"It was clear we would lose the battle. Then something—I'm not sure what—happened, and the enemy started to flee."

Egrith continues to cry.

He hesitates. "After their soldiers scattered, we searched for Argo, and when we found him he was already dead." Gareth takes her in his arms again and holds her as she wails. After a long while she calms down, and he walks her to her bed. "His remains are being sent to Martoldt Hall. And this—for you—was in a pocket under his leathers." He hands her a folded piece of parchment.

"I can't bear it now," she says, and places it under her pillow.

"I'll stay until Grena comes. You shouldn't be alone."

She nods.

Gareth sits next to her as she burrows under the covers and continues to cry. He takes her hand. Exhausted from sobbing she drifts off to sleep, the pillow wet from her tears. Far into the night, she awakens to the glow from a candle and sees Grena dozing in the chair by the window. She rolls over and sleeps again.

A cool sensation on her face startles her and she flinches.

"It's alright, Child," Grena says, and removes her hand from Egrith's forehead.

Light streams through the window and Egrith puts the pillow over her head.

"You're feverish. I'll close the drapes and bring a damp cloth."

Egrith ventures out from under the pillow and Grena places the cool cloth above her eyes.

"Thank you," Egrith says, and sits up.

"I spoke with your brother." Grena takes her hand.

"He told you."

"Yes. I am very sorry for you, Dear. But you must go on, and regain your strength. Someday, you'll fall in love again. The King—"

"I will never speak to Father again."

"King Egad loves you, in spite of his actions."

"He took my child, then Argo," Egrith says. She leaves her bed and moves to the window. "I shall never see him again."

"Prince Gareth said there was a letter," Grena says.

"I haven't had the courage to read it."

"It might soothe you."

Egrith sighs, and tears form in her eyes again. "It's under my pillow."

"Do you want me to read it to you?"

She nods and sits by the window.

Grena finds the letter and pulls a chair next to Egrith's. She hands Egrith the parchment and opens it. A small bundle of cloth falls out. Grena stoops to pick it up but Egrith moves faster. She unfolds the cloth. A silver sapphire ring drops into her lap.

"Beautiful," Egrith says, and holds the ring up in the light. She slips it on her right hand. "Will you please read the letter now?"

"My dearest Egrith. I cannot say if and when we shall see one another again. I hold hope in my heart for that day. Perhaps your father will come to terms with his anger, and allow us to meet. I love you, and our child. I have always loved you. This ring has been in my family for generations. I give it to you as a token of our love, with hope you will wear it with joy in your heart. Be brave, my dearest love. In this life or the next, we shall be happy again." Grena's voice shakes as she tries not to weep. "I am forever yours, Argo."

Egrith stares out the window, and then rises and opens it. She places her hands on the sill and glances down toward the ground, then at the sky.

"Come away from there," Grena says. "It's still chilly."

"I'm hot. And the sky is so blue." She sighs. "Blue, like this ring when the sun shines on it."

"The storm passed. Egrith, dear, it is time to live again."

Egrith blinks tears away and brightens. "Yes. I'll be alright. You can go now, my Grena. Just leave supper outside the door. I think I need rest today."

"As you wish, my sweet girl." Grena moves towards the door with a quick glance at Egrith before she leaves.

Egrith reads the letter over and over. It becomes crumpled and stained with her tears. She holds her hand up so the ring can sparkle in the sun's light. Later, the sun fades as night approaches. She gets into bed. Sleep won't come, so she rises and lights a candle, then opens the window. "Nice and cool," she says, and watches the flicker of Riverton's lights below. "My daughter. I would give anything to see you."

She paces, remembering Argo's kisses and their meetings in the secret chamber beyond Grandmama's wardrobe. She forgets supper waits outside her door. The ring is heavy on her finger and she rubs the sapphire stone. "Beautiful," she says again, and tears come once more. "This dread in my stomach. It will never pass."

Egrith sees her reflection in the mirror, starts to brush her hair but lets it fall around her face instead. She removes her necklace and it drops to the floor; the sound of its clink on the stone startles her. She glances over her shoulder and when she turns back to the mirror, she imagines she sees the three women who threatened to take her child, and she squeezes her eyes shut. When she opens them again the women are gone.

Egrith shudders, and paces about the chamber again.

She thinks of the people she loves. Grena. Gareth. Loren. Dirk. Teurith, the child she'll never know. And now, she will never see Argo. "Not in this world." She cries, and moves to the window. High above Riverton, Egrith sits on the sill. "All I have to do is swing my legs over and let myself fall."

But she doesn't. She stands and paces, walking in circles around the chamber. "No relief." She rubs her stomach as she walks. "Gareth and Loren have each other. Grena will always be there, a sweet constant in our lives." She reads Argo's letter. "My Argo. I will never love another. Too painful, too much sorrow."

The pacing tires Egrith, yet she continues. "I wish I could join you." Round and round the room she circles, past the window, her armoire, the bed, the door. Then finally she pauses and sobs anew, her body trembling with anguish. "When we die do we see the living?" she wonders. Her heart sinks even more with despair. "Wait." She moves to her dresser and opens her trinket box, and takes the statuette of Queen Benadras, her sapphire eyes sparkling in the candle light. "For my daughter." She moves to her writing desk and takes a quill and some parchment from the drawer. She pauses when she sees the letter opener. Then she shuts the drawer and starts writing.

She writes of her love for those close to her, and thanks them. She writes of her love for Argo. She writes for her daughter with the hope that she'll know how much her mother loved her. After a while Egrith stops writing. She leaves the letter on the desk with the statuette for her daughter. The window is still open. She leans out and scans the ground below. "Long way down. How horrible it would be if…" She returns to the desk and opens the drawer. The letter opener reflects the candlelight. Egrith pricks her finger on the tip of the blade; its sharpness surprises her.

"Not too many choices now." Her body ripples with chills. She takes the letter opener with her and sits in the chair by the window, then sighs. Relief washes over her. "Too much suffering, but no more," she says. With hope for peace, she turns her hands, palms facing up, and examines the veins on her wrists. She pushes the long velvety sleeves of her dress up. Without hesitation she cuts, quick and clean, from where the vein starts to the top of the wrist. Blood runs out, and drips in her lap. Before she loses strength, she slices the other wrist.

Egrith smiles, and relaxes into the cushioned chair. As the life begins to drain from her body the room grows brighter. She sees a field with tall grass waving in the wind. A dog barks, and laughter drifts to her on the breeze. Argo and a young girl, who looks much like Egrith, run as the dog chases them around the field. "Wait for me," Egrith says. Argo sees her and runs towards her with outstretched arms. The girl and dog disappear into the background as Argo reaches Egrith and embraces her. Egrith melts in his arms; her suffering slips away.

# XXIII
## *The Battle of Barkus Wall*
### *The Year 549*

Thousands of hooves thunder up the hill from Lord Frolichen's encampment. Teurith steadies her nerves as she waits with Djáraad and the soldiers of Third Battalion. Commander Smyth and the archers of Second Battalion, flanked by the cavalries of Lord Krimpt's First and Lord Tannen's Fifth wait in front of Djáraad's men. The swordsmen of Fourth under Lord Tomas stand poised at the rear of the army.

Djáraad shouts orders. "Ready the star-discs."

Teurith opens the pouch at her waist.

"Nock arrows," Commander Smyth bellows at the archers of Second Battalion.

The enemy's cavalry slows as it approaches the opening in Barkus Wall, then files through in small groups. Their riders charge once they've breached the wall and advance toward King Gareth's army.

"Loose," Commander Smyth yells, and hundreds of arrows whiz through the air at the enemy horsemen. Some horses fall and their riders scramble to recover. Lord Krimpt and Lord Tannen lead their cavalries at the enemy.

Frolichen's fallen litter the hill, but more of their troops stream through the wall's opening. Lords Tannen and Krimpt assault with their battalions toward Barkus Wall, trampling enemy soldiers underfoot. Lord Krimpt's sword gleams in the light as he fells enemy men, the jewels on the hilt glowing with magic. Once King Gareth's riders reach the wall Frolichen's archers fire on them and they're forced to circle up the hill and prepare for another attack.

Teurith moves through the troops as they open their pouches with the star-discs. "Ready," she cries as loud as she can, and the soldiers obey, waiting for her command to let the them fly. As Frolichen's remaining warriors near them, Teurith yells, "Now." Enemy stragglers stagger and fall, discs embedded in their foreheads.

Teurith catches sight of Djáraad as Third Battalion regroups. He cries, "Battering rams!" Large portions of the wall crumble, leaving room for the enemy cavalry to attack in greater numbers. King Gareth's cavalries charge again where gaps in the wall are widest, trying to keep up with the sheer numbers approaching.

Djáraad moves next to Teurith. "They don't even care if they're going to die," he says, as they watch enemy men fall. "They'll soon wear us down."

Enemy hordes push King Gareth's forces farther up the hill. Foot soldiers prepare for hand-to-hand combat, swords at the ready.

Beyond the wall to the south enemy troops with red banners part for a rider with a red-plumed helmet. The hordes pound their spears on the ground and chant. "FANG-thar, FANG-thar, FANG-thar." Fangthar charges and his throng of soldiers follows.

"The Teeth," Teurith cries.

Djáraad turns to her. "Call the Gördög again. We don't have a chance if she doesn't come." Teurith races beyond the melee to the hilltop. With a final look at the battle raging below, she heads north through the camp until she reaches the other side of the hill.

*Silva.* Teurith roams down the grassy incline, calling to the Gördög. She scans the skies, although she knows Silva is only visible when on the ground. The wind carries the sounds of battle to her and she worries. *Silva.* The ground soon shudders and Teurith turns. Then, the air shimmers. "Silva." Teurith runs toward her friend. "I knew you'd come. Thank you."

*Time is short. Hurry.*

Silva lowers her head and Teurith climbs on her neck. "Wait, just a moment." Teurith removes the stone from the pack, and grasps it to her bosom. "Ready." Silva heaves a sigh, lopes forward and takes off.

They fly over the top of the hill and Teurith scans the battleground below. King

Gareth's army remains on the north side of the wall, and Lord Frolichen's forces continue to advance, their hordes blanketing the plains south of the wall. She sees The Teeth cutting through the throng of soldiers, towards her Uncle Gareth.

"We must help them," Teurith shouts, over the whooshing sound of Silva's wings. They circle above where her Uncle Gareth's cavalries and enemy horsemen fight. Teurith sees the King caught in the midst of the fray. "Silva!"

The Gördög swoops down over Frolichen's riders, the roaring sound of her wings distracting them from King Gareth and his men. Horsemen from both sides scatter, and leave room for the King's men to retreat up the hill.

The Teeth follows, undaunted.

*The King cannot hold them off. Call the ghost army. Now.*

Teurith rubs the smooth center of the stone. "Please. Help us."

The stone warms in her hands, and the sky above darkens. As the sun fades, the stone radiates an eerie orange light, then bursts with color. Ghosts from the dead soldier's Army of the Fallen surge into the sky. Their energy focuses and they pour down upon Lord Frolichen's forces.

Screams from the enemy echo through the darkness. Men screech as the ghosts pass through their bodies, striking fear in their souls. Soldiers drop their weapons and remove their armor, clawing at their skin as if stinging insects cover their bodies. Others bleed from their eyes and ears, blinded and screaming from the pain. Men fall as their hearts stop beating. The ghostly Fallen destroy the enemy north of the wall, then move south, an immense cloud of dust in their wake.

Silva flies over the wall and Teurith looks to the south. As enemy troops disappear, she sees a rider fleeing in the distance, the red plume on his helmet visible. "Silva. We have to take him down. He mustn't escape."

*Be wary, Teurith.*

Silva circles the rider, and starts to materialize as she prepares to land.

Fangthar faces them.

As Silva and Teurith near him he takes off his helmet and leers, his jagged teeth visible, a spear in his right hand poised to throw.

Silva tries to move out of his range.

The Teeth lets the spear fly.

As Teurith begins to dismount she hears the spear whir over her shoulder and it slams into the Gördög's head.

"Silva!" Teurith screams.

The Gördög falters.

Teurith grasps Silva's fur and the Gördög collapses on the ground. Teurith slides off Silva's neck and strokes her mammoth face.

The Gördög shudders, her breathing labored.

"Oh, my friend." Teurith drops the stone and buries her face in the Gördög's fur.

*Teurith. Be on guard.*

She turns to the sound of approaching hooves.

Fangthar slows his horse and stops at a distance. His laughter carries over the empty plains. "All alone, aren't we?" He takes something from off of his saddle. He holds a severed head above him. "A friend of yours, perhaps?"

Teurith shivers.

Tomas' head dangles by his hair in Fangthar's hand.

The Teeth laughs again.

Anger explodes in Teurith's mind. She discards her leather shirt, revealing the chainmail with its gems shining in the sunlight. She stands her ground.

"That won't protect you." Fangthar continues to leer.

Aware of the pouch at her waist Teurith knows she has one star-disc left.

Fangthar's horse knickers and stomps.

The Teeth drops Tomas' head and charges at her, his sword raised above him.

Teurith pulls the disc from the pouch.

A woman's laughter carries over the plains.

Chills ripple up Teurith's spine, as the one woman's laughter becomes two, then three. Teurith freezes.

Fangthar gallops closer.

Teurith's anger rekindles. She takes the star-disc. With a snap of her wrist, the disc strikes Fangthar's horse in the eye.

The horse screams and throws Fangthar to the ground. He soon rises, his open mouth revealing the sharp, pointed teeth. He smiles and walks towards her.

She stoops and grabs the stone. It pulsates in her hands.

"Give it to me," Fangthar hisses.

The ground rumbles and the three witch-women appear behind him.

"No," Teurith whispers, her hands shaking.

He steps closer. "We will spare you, if you do."

*Teurith. The stone.*

Silva's voice, although weak, brings Teurith to attention.

*Your father.*

Teurith concentrates.

The stone warms in Teurith's hands, becoming so hot she drops it.

Fangthar lunges toward the stone.

The witch-women cackle again as Teurith stays between the stone and the Teeth.

"Father," Teurith calls, and stands aside.

A fierce wind kicks up.

Before Fangthar reaches the stone, it expands. The shade of Teurith's father, Lord Argo, emerges from it. The wind rushes over the plains and knocks Fangthar to the ground. Argo's ghostly form looms large and menacing.

The witch-women wail, then disappear.

Lord Argo shrieks and approaches Fangthar.

Teurith watches The Teeth cower in her father Argo's shadow.

Lord Argo rips Fangthar's helmet off his head, grabs him by his hair and drags him toward the stone.

"No," Fangthar cries.

Lord Argo glances toward his daughter once, then disappears into the stone with Fangthar, his voice trailing behind him. "Teurith, my brave daughter, help us."

Teurith can't move. For a long while she stays still as the sound of the wind howling around her dies down. Finally, she notices the stone, now returned to its normal size. She picks it up and holds it to her chest. And she remembers.

"Silva." She runs to the Gördög and rests her head against Silva's neck. Teurith releases her tears. She cries for the Gördög, for Tomas, for her fathers, both Dirk and Argo, and for her mother, Egrith. "Silva?" Teurith strokes the side of the beast's head.

Nothing.

"Oh, my dear Silva." Teurith can't cry anymore. "Thank you, my friend." She slides to the ground next to the Gördög with the stone clutched in her hands, then she drifts off to sleep to the sound of horses running in the distance.

"Teurith, try to drink this," a voice says.

Her eyes flutter. She closes them again.

"…fever, she's so warm."

"Try to sit her up," Dirk says.

"We shouldn't force her. Maybe—"

Teurith awakens and looks around her, frantic.

"Dear Child, you're safe," King Gareth says.

Dirk stands over his daughter and stoops to smooth hair out of her eyes.

"Father?" she says.

"I'm here, Teury."

"Silva, and Tomas—they're dead." She cries into Dirk's shoulder.

"We must let her sleep. She's overwrought," King Gareth says.

Teurith rubs her eyes and her surroundings come into focus. In the King's tent, Uncle Gareth, Dirk and Djáraad stand over her. She tries to get up. Djáraad helps her adjust the pillows so she can see everyone.

"What happened?" she says. "How did Tomas—and Silva—" Tears form in her eyes.

Djáraad speaks first. "Fangthar. The Teeth. He killed Tomas."

"Yes," she says.

"Fangthar assaulted us on horseback, killing many good men. I couldn't hold him off and when he was about to strike me down Tomas stepped in with two other soldiers and beat him back. Then Fangthar charged again and the force of his horse racing toward Tomas was enough for the Teeth to sever Tomas' head. Tomas lost his life defending me." Djáraad takes a deep breath. "Then Fangthar fled south before the ghost army could get to him."

"I have to stand," Teurith says.

Dirk helps her up and embraces her. "There, my brave girl."

Djáraad says, "We should ride and find Fangthar else he'll come back to haunt us."

King Gareth nods. "I agree. We'll form a special company and—"

"He's gone," Teurith says.

"How?" the King says.

Teurith shudders. "He found me. He—he killed Silva, and then came at me. But I took the stone and…" She looks at her father, Dirk, then continues. "I took the stone and called father—the warrior Lord Argo—and he saved me, then pulled The Teeth through the stone with him and they disappeared. And Silva. We should do something for her, a ritual burning."

Djáraad looks to King Gareth and Dirk and they nod. "Teurith. After we found you with Silva your father carried you to his horse. As we were about to leave to get you to safety, the clouds parted and the sun shone on Silva. We heard the sound of wings above and she rose up into the sun's beam. Something lifted her higher until she faded into the light."

"We believe she rests now, in a place of infinite healing," King Gareth says.

Teurith's eyes fill again. Her father hugs her and she pulls away. "But the stone, where is it?"

"In your pack," Djáraad says. He stoops and hands her the rucksack.

"Thank you," she says, and sighs. "The Teeth—Fangthar—was going to take it from me. Then Argo came and—wait—Argo said something as he disappeared."

"What?" Djáraad says.

"He said…" Teurith takes the stone from her pack, and it glows.

In the dimness of King Gareth's tent, images appear before them. Teurith steps back with Dirk, Djáraad and her uncle. They watch as a large battle comes into focus, then hones in on a scene.

"There's my father," King Gareth says.

They see King Egad stare as a young Gareth cradles Argo's lifeless body in his lap.

"Argo," Gareth says. "His death. And my father did not care."

Teurith takes her uncle's hand as the scene unfolds. Young Gareth stands, approaches King Egad and they have heated words as the distant sounds of battle resonate around them. King Egad storms away and Gareth returns to Argo. Teurith sees her uncle mourn the loss of his friend.

Then Argo gazes through the stone, across time, straight at her. Teurith steps back. *Help us, he says.*

"I have to go," she says, and pulls her hand out of her uncle's.

"Where?" Dirk says.

"I must help them."

"No," King Gareth says.

"If I don't go, they'll all die, and—"

"We cannot afford to lose you as well."

King Gareth takes her arm and she wrenches free. Before anyone can stop her, she moves to the stone. It widens for her. She steps into it and disappears.

# XXIV
## *The Son of the Father*
### *The Years 533/549*

Swirling energy pulls Teurith through the stone and into a tunnel. Green and blue lights cascade around her as the energies propel her toward a white light at the end. She sees smiling faces of her loved ones ahead. The tugging sensation intensifies and she flies faster. Her mother, Egrith. Tomas. Her Great-Grandmama. Silva, the Gördög. Her father, Argo. She stretches her arms out as she approaches them.

Then, they disappear, and darkness surrounds Teurith.

For a moment, she panics; her body floats in a murky void. Sudden, flashing colors blind her and she topples to the ground. She finds herself in the midst of soldiers fighting, dead bodies strewn about her. The stone, clutched in her hands, flashes. She scrambles to a safer place, away from the melee, and sees her Uncle Gareth holding Argo close to him. Argo struggles to breathe.

"Come, Gareth. Before they surround us," King Egad calls from astride his horse.

"I won't let him die alone," Gareth shouts, his face twisted with anger and pain.

"Very well," King Egad says, a scowl on his face. He pulls his visor down and moves into the throng, his sword slashing left and right at enemy soldiers.

Fangthar's men surround Uncle Gareth and Argo and they close in on the two friends. What is left of the King's army cannot hold them off. Gareth stands and draws his sword.

"Uncle Gareth," Teurith calls as loud as she can.

He glances around at the sound of her voice, but doesn't see her. With his sword poised to fight he keeps himself in front of his friend Argo.

The stone warms in her hand, becoming so hot she almost drops it. The clouds part and the sun shines down on the battlefield. Teurith angles the stone to catch the sun's light; it turns a fiery orange color, and she directs the light into the melee. The orangey beam focuses on opposing soldiers and King Egad's men scatter.

Enemy men scream, and try to remove their armor. Teurith sees their skin blister in the light reflected from the stone. Some of their armor melts before they can take it off, the yellow and black scorpion sigils on their breastplates dissipating into the molten metal. Shrieks reverberate over the plains as enemy soldiers disintegrate into puddles of magma.

Teurith's Uncle Gareth sits with Argo again, tears streaming down Gareth's battle-worn face leaving thin trails of dirt and ash. With the enemy's men destroyed, he sobs his grief into the hot air. He holds Argo close until his anguish is spent. Gareth pulls Argo's lifeless body up from where he lay and carries him, sidestepping the dead as he walks from the scene.

Sunlight fades and darkness spreads over the fields. The only light left radiates from the stone resting in Teurith's lap. She tries to stand and can't. Soldiers from both sides are gone, or dead. She shivers, and manages to rise by pushing herself off the ground with her hands, then walks through her exhaustion, aimless, without direction.

She weeps for her father, Argo, for Uncle Gareth and his grief. She cries for her father, Dirk, who bore the weight of secrets he could not tell. After she wanders for a long while, the wind shifts and she smells the ocean, then follows its scent until she comes to the place where soft sand meets the sea.

Teurith clutches the stone. It continues to glow until the moon rises over the ocean. Far away from the battlefield, she sits on the sand and watches the ebb and flow of the tide. She thinks of her mother, who died so young. She curls up and cries herself to sleep.

"Teurith," a distant voice calls.

She stretches and turns on her side.

"Wake up, my Love."

Teurith opens her eyes. The misty dawn is almost quiet. She hears the gentle lapping of waves on the beach. And the voice. "Hello?" she says. She feels the stone's smooth center, and it widens once again. The sound of laughter carries over the sand. She rubs her eyes.

"Teurith." A young woman materializes, her long black hair blowing in the breeze. "My beautiful daughter," she says, and stretches her hand out.

Teurith grasps it. "Mother."

"We haven't much time. You're beginning to fade from the time where you belong."

"But—"

"Come."

Arm in arm they float over the ocean, then through the lavender and pink of the sunrise. Teurith's heart soars at the sound of her mother's soft laughter. Wisps of their hair commingle as they move farther away from the shoreline.

"I've never been so happy," Teurith says.

"You deserve to be, my dear Child. You saved the Realm. Twice."

"I suppose so; it all seems so hazy now."

Her mother laughs again, like faery bells tinkling. "Yes, you did. It'll all come back to you over time. You have always been our hope." She takes her daughter's hand and squeezes it.

Teurith smiles into the wind, the salty air damp and fragrant. Her mother's grasp on her hand weakens. "Mother?"

"I must go. Find your way, my Sweet." She fades.

Teurith clutches at the air, then feels herself falling. *Mother!* She swims in a thick darkness, and can't catch her breath.

She hears whimpering, and then feels Argo the dog nuzzling at her ear.

"Teury?"

In the dark, Teurith continues to gasp for air. Argo whines. Then, a firm hand on her shoulder shakes her.

"Mother, where are you?" Teurith murmurs.

"Teury, all is well," Dirk's voice says.

She struggles to open her eyes. "Father."

Dirk helps her sit up.

"Mother. I was with her. And she led me back. She was so beautiful and kind."

"It was just a dream, dear Girl," Dirk says.

"No. It wasn't, I—"

"She's right," King Gareth says and turns to Teurith. "You disappeared."

"So much happened. I saw you, Uncle Gareth, and—the warrior Argo—and King Egad fled. Then you were cornered and I didn't know what to do so I took the stone and it—killed them."

"Yes," King Gareth says. "Something happened. I remember parts of it now. Somehow, the Battle of Sounding Sea Fortress ended to our advantage. Teurith and her stone saved us, although it didn't happen without great loss." He steps out of the tent and returns with Djáraad, Lord Tannen and Lord Krimpt.

Djáraad moves toward Teurith and she runs to hug him. "I'm happy you're safe," he says.

She kisses his cheek before returning to Dirk's side.

King Gareth addresses his commanders. "Lord Tannen. I am sorry for your loss. Tomas is our loss as well, a good soldier. He was a bright hope for our future."

"Thank you, my King," Tannen says.

"I want you to know we have Teurith to thank for surviving this battle. We live because of her bravery. But we cannot afford to celebrate now. Djáraad, ready your troops for departure. Tannen, Krimpt, Commander Smyth, prepare yours. We head for Riverton early."

They nod and leave.

"Now there is the other matter—of my sister Margrin and her son," the King says, and glances at Teurith. "They should ride under guard in one of the wagons until we can get them home. Dirk, please care for our Teurith. See that she rests. I must attend to Margrin for now." He walks Dirk and Teurith to their tent, Argo the dog following close behind.

Dirk drapes a blanket over Teurith once she's settled on pillows in her corner of their tent. "I understand you can't quite eat yet, but tomorrow you must break your fast before we travel." He stoops to kiss her forehead.

"I will."

Teurith watches the candle from the lantern flicker and cast shadows on the tent's ceiling. Sleep eludes her. She thinks of her Aunt Margrin and tries to imagine what she's like, maybe similar to her sister Egrith. And her son, Teurith's cousin. Who was his father? Perhaps he never knew his father, like Teurith. She yawns, and dozes off.

*She shows the boy the crystal and he snatches it from her hand. "It's alright. Hold it up in the light," she says. A small rabbit forages in the corner of the courtyard. The boy raises his arm and catches light from the sun in the crystal. He shines the beam on the rabbit. For a moment, the rabbit goes about her business. Then, she squeals as smoke curls off the fur on her rump. She hops into a shaded bush and disappears. The boy laughs. Teurith's eyes widen. "You mustn't do things like that. Poor creature." The boy hangs his head in an effort to hide his smile. "I didn't mean anything by it," he says.*

Teurith wakes, and rubs sweat off her brow. Argo lifts his head, then rests it on her foot. Her dog and Dirk's snoring reassure her, and she drifts off to sleep until Dirk rouses her at first light. She stretches and splashes water on her face. Outside the tent, she sees troops already in formation, preparing for the march north.

"The ride back to Riverton shouldn't take as long. But carts that once carried grain now bear our dead. Stay close, Teury," Dirk says.

"Yes, Father."

Teurith sits beside Dirk on the wagon, Argo resting at their feet. They don't speak much, both exhausted from ordeals of battle and loss. At the end of each travel day, Teurith sleeps until the following morning. On the third day, they see the amethyst-colored turrets of Riverton Castle in the distance, shining in the noon sun.

"Father, look," Teurith says.

"A sight to behold. Teury. I know you've slept well during the journey. You need more rest."

Teurith allows herself to smile.

Dirk slows the carthorses and stops by the main entrance to the castle. "Look, there's Grena," he says.

Teurith jumps down from the wagon and runs into Grena's arms, hugging her until Grena steps back.

"Goodness, child. I'll have someone draw you a bath," she says. "Oh, it's wonderful to see you."

"Nice to see you, too. But can I look for Djáraad first?"

"I think he'll be even happier to visit if you bathe beforehand," Grena says. "I must see to your Aunt Margrin and her son."

Teurith sighs and watches Grena bustle away, then walks through the castle's hallways, which hum with excitement at the return of King Gareth's army. Her stomach flips with anticipation as she thinks of Djáraad. Then her mood shifts. *Tomas.* Wrenn will be devastated.

She passes a group of servants huddling around a girl in their midst. They notice Teurith, stop consoling their friend and curtsy.

"Please don't do that. Care for your friend."

"Her love didna come back," one of the girls says.

*So much death.*

Teurith approaches the girl and embraces her. "I'm very sorry for your loss."

She leaves them and continues through the hallways, slowing her pace as she passes one of the castle courtyards. She remembers her recent dream of the cruel boy, and shivers, then shakes off the recollection.

After her bath Teurith brushes her hair, finally free of tangles, and thinks of her mother. She examines the hairbrush and feels its smooth pearl handle, once held by her mother. Teurith sits in the chair by the window. Argo comes and puts his paw on the arm of the chair. "Good, good dog," Teurith says, and caresses his soft fur until she finally curls herself up in the chair and falls asleep.

She wakes up at sunset to the sound of someone knocking. Her eyes adjust to the dimness and she answers the door. Her uncle stands before her.

"Teurith, you've been crying," he says, and they embrace. "I know you're tired and have been through so much. You're needed in the Great Hall, and I wanted to come and get you myself."

"What is it?" she says.

"Wash your face and I'll explain as we walk."

Teurith washes and smooths wrinkles from her dress, then follows the King out the door. They stroll a few minutes in silence until he speaks.

"Teurith. While you're the clear successor to the throne, you have a cousin who is next in line, after you."

"Aunt Margrin's son?"

"Yes. Your aunt is very ill, and hasn't spoken since they sent her to us. We suspect she was not treated well over the years, to say the least. But her son…" King Gareth begins, then pauses.

"What about him?"

King Gareth stops and faces her with his hands on her shoulders. "Teurith." He lowers his voice. "There is something—not right—about him. At first, I thought I'd give you the task of showing him around as a companion. But now I believe he should begin his training immediately and live in the barracks. Tonight, I will introduce him to the court, and that includes you. But after, please avoid him."

"And—his father?"

"That is a conversation for another time."

"But what about my training?" Teurith says.

"In addition to Djáraad's duties as commander of Third Battalion, he will work with you personally and hone your skills." Her Uncle Gareth smiles. "I suspect he won't mind."

"Thank you, Uncle."

"Teurith. There's one more thing. Keep the stone hidden."

She nods and they continue walking.

They reach the hall and the steward announces them.

"King Gareth, and his niece, the Princess Teurith."

Every person kneels before the King and Teurith, with one exception.

King Gareth frowns. "I will now introduce a new addition to our court. My sister Margrin's son, my nephew, Segrimond."

Segrimond inclines his head.

Teurith meets his gaze and shudders. *The boy from her dreams.* She manages to look away.

The King continues. "And now, we celebrate with feasting. Let us have music."

Musicians play in the background as celebrants mill about, talking and greeting one another, then they seat themselves for the feast.

Teurith's eyes tire as the evening of celebration wears on. When people finally begin to retire, she rises and approaches Djáraad.

He takes her arm and leads her to a corner of the hall. "Do you want to get out of here?" he says.

"I'd love to."

They move through corridors, heading for the courtyard where they usually meet. As they turn a corner Djáraad's hand bumps into Teurith's. He pulls it back. She pauses for a moment, then hurries forward, takes his hand in hers and they move faster. The deserted courtyard welcomes them with the fragrance of flowers and moonlight. They move to the bench in the corner and sit.

Teurith releases Djáraad's hand and faces him. "Uncle Gareth says I am to train with only you. Is this alright?"

"Of course," he says.

She places her hand on his arm. He removes it and instead, holds it in his, squeezing too hard.

"Ow. What's the matter?" she says.

"I have something to tell you."

She smiles at his somber tone. "It can't be that bad. We won the battle." Then her face darkens. "I'm sorry about Tomas. It was thoughtless of me to make light."

"Yes. He was my friend. But it's not only that."

"Then, what?"

Djáraad looks toward the courtyard entrance. "It's that boy."

Teurith grimaces. "I know. Uncle already told me."

He hesitates. "I'm not supposed to say this. But I worry for you."

"I'm grateful for your concern, my Friend. What is it?"

"Segrimond has his eye on the throne. I saw him glaring at you. I do not trust him."

"Uncle Gareth implied this when we spoke, and will send Segrimond to the barracks."

"There's more." He touches her cheek with the back of his hand.

Teurith relaxes, and waits.

"It's—his father."

"He has a father? Alive?"

"No." Djáraad places his arm around her shoulders and holds her close.

"Then what could be wrong?" she says.

"Segrimond is an offspring of violence. His father, Lord Fengan, raped and abused your Aunt Margrin for many years."

Teurith pulls away. "Lord Fengan…"

"We know him as Fangthar—The Teeth."

"How horrible. My poor aunt," she cries.

"I wasn't supposed to tell you. Segrimond is his father's son. I see that already."

Teurith tells Djáraad about her dream of the boy's cruelty.

He kisses her forehead and whispers in her ear. "I will always be here with you."

She tries to smile. "I know." She pulls his arms around her and kisses him on the mouth.

He hesitates.

"It's alright." She kisses him again.

They embrace long into the night, until the moonlight passes beyond the courtyard walls and they're left in darkness.

Made in the USA
Middletown, DE
12 September 2022

10252430R00099